ON THE RISE

H.K. CHRISTIE

This is a work of fiction. Names, characters, businesses, places, events and incidents are either the products of the author's imagination or used in a fictitious manner. Any resemblance to actual persons, living or dead, or actual events is purely coincidental.

ALSO BY H.K. CHRISTIE

The Selena Bailey Novella Series

If you like thrilling twists, dark tension, and smart and driven women, then you'll love this suspenseful series featuring a young Selena Bailey and her turbulent path to becoming a top notch kickass private investigator.

Not Like Her, Book 1

One In Five, Book 2

On The Rise, Book 3

The Unbreakable Series

The Unbreakable Series is a heart-warming women's fiction series, inspired by true events. If you like journeys of self-discovery, wounded heroines, and laugh-or-cry moments, you'll love the Unbreakable series.

We Can't Be Broken, Book 0

Where I'm Supposed To Be, Book 1

Change of Plans, Book 2

For Mr. Christie

1

"I promise I won't let you down!" Selena hung up the phone and dropped it onto her desk. *Finally.* Her stepmother, Martina, had agreed to let her take the lead on a missing persons case. Since she started working part-time at Martina's security and investigations firm, Selena's involvement had been mostly limited to mind-numbing activities like reviewing endless pages of phone records and watching security footage until she thought her eyes would bleed and her brain would melt.

Sure, in the last six months Martina had let her tag along on a few stakeouts, but those were few and far between. But now, eighteen months after she had started working at Drakos Monroe Security and Investigations, she was going to be able to prove to Martina and the rest of the team she wasn't just some annoying college kid allowed into the firm due to her status as the stepdaughter of one of the partners. She would not only find out what happened to the missing seven-year-old girl, but she'd do it in record time.

Of course, Martina had cautioned Selena that she would be required to report her every move to Martina, since it was her first *official* case and all. As much as she hated the idea of being babysat, she supposed it was a necessary rite of passage on her path to becoming a licensed private investigator. Not that she was sure her final career choice would be a PI over a career in law enforcement, but either way she figured if she could do the private investigator thing while still in college, why not?

It didn't even bother Selena that she was likely given the case because all of the other investigators were tied up on other work and the clients had pleaded for Drakos Monroe to accept their case even if it was to be investigated by a junior investigator. Selena knew when to seize an opportunity when it was presented.

Dang. She was just glad Martina had agreed to let her have the opportunity. Over the holidays, Selena had spent most of the break trying to convince her stepmother she could handle more than reviewing records at a desk. It was the same old fight. Martina was concerned that Selena should be focusing on her studies and not on leading investigations. Selena had been adamant that she could handle both school and work. She had a pretty good handle on her sophomore year as a Criminal Justice major at San Francisco University. She had found her groove pretty early on in college and had received all A's and A-'s her first year—and that was while she was running her own secret operation to take down a fraternity house that was known for sexually assaulting women. *Please.* She was more than confident she could handle a little more responsibility at the firm.

The one thing that took up more time in college than she'd ever expected was her boyfriend, Brendon. He was unexpected in more than one way. She never thought she'd want to have another boyfriend after a dangerous romance while she was a senior in high school. But Brendon had proven to her over the last year that some boyfriends were sweet and kind and could bring a spark of happiness to your already great life. Not *all* men were monsters.

She couldn't wait to tell her college BFF and roommate, Dee, that she would be leading her first investigation. She was so psyched she wanted to turn up the stereo and dance a jig around her cramped room, but she wouldn't get very far. The room barely had space for her twin bed, her bookshelf, and her desk. She may not be able to dance in the room, but she had lucked out since her writing desk fit perfectly below a drafty old window that had views of the ocean.

The sound of the front door creaking open made her body grow rigid. She grabbed her baton from on top of her desk and assumed a fighting stance.

Since moving off campus, she'd regressed a bit in her ability to relax at home. In the dorm there was one entrance and exit; in the two-story rental she and Dee shared with three other students from the university, there were several points of entry. The funky old house in San Francisco's Sunset District was only four blocks from the ocean and she loved it, even if it made her *a bit* more anxious.

Not only that, but living with a group of other college students made Selena feel like a typical nineteen-year-old. It was comforting since in so many ways her life up until that point had been anything but typical. She never thought she could be totally normal, but hosting parties and having a boyfriend and a bestie in college was more normal than she ever thought she'd be.

Selena slowly stepped out of her bedroom and headed down the hall to the living room, baton extended. She called out, "Dee?"

Dee stood in the entry still wearing her down jacket and scarf, sifting through mail on the banister, before glancing up. "Hey, girl. Sorry, I should've called out."

Selena's body relaxed and she retracted the baton and slipped it into her pocket. "Hey. Guess what?" Selena went on to tell her the good news about finally be able to work a real investigation.

"That's super cool. Who is the missing girl? Are they from around here?"

"They live in San Bruno. The only details I have are that the girl went missing from a nail salon, but the police found no trace of her ever being there and so suspicion moved to the parents. The parents hired us to not only prove their innocence but to locate their daughter. I meet with the clients tomorrow and will get the full details."

Dee unwound her wool scarf and hung it on the hook in the hallway before ruffling her fingers through her shoulder-length blond hair. "Wow. That's serious. Martina gave you full lead?"

Selena smirked. "Mostly. I'm official lead, but I will be working pretty close with Martina."

"Well, good luck. I hope you find out what happened to the girl." Dee's face twisted. "Ugh. There are so many creeps out there."

"Ain't that the truth."

Dee would know, she was a survivor. Selena had been impressed by Dee and how she'd turned her tragedy into something positive. After being sexually assaulted their first semester at SFU, Dee had started counseling and attended the on-campus Center for Victims of Sexual Violence support group each week. Then she took it a step further and started volunteering at the center. Dee explained that she wanted her attack to mean something, instead of it being just another senseless act of violence. Selena admired her strength and positive outlook.

"Have you had dinner yet?" Selena asked.

"No, not yet. I haven't shopped either. I'm afraid that I'll be eating Pop-Tarts for dinner."

Selena shook her head at Dee. It was a wonder how Dee stayed so thin. "That would be a terrible dinner. I need to pick up a few things at the store too. You want to go shopping and maybe grab dinner from the salad bar at the grocery store?"

Dee nodded. "Sounds like a plan."

Selena had started self-defense and weapons training with Martina two years ago after she'd been kidnapped by her psycho ex. During that time, her stepmother had drilled into her that a healthy diet was essential to being physically fit and ready for a fight. *Strong body, strong mind.* Selena had eventually given in to the idea and now attempted to limit her sugar intake and eat mostly whole foods like lean protein and fresh fruits and veggies. It was a slow, *painful* transition. But Martina had been right, and Selena felt better both mentally and physically than she had ever felt in her nearly twenty years on the planet.

Almost dying made her realize that life was precious and that she needed to live her life in the best way she could. She was still almost a year away from being eligible to apply for her private investigator's license. Luckily, she was getting a lot of hours working at the firm, but she couldn't wait for when she could get her license. Assuming she didn't screw up this new investigation and could get a recommendation from Martina. *Selena Bailey, Private Investigator.* Oh, how she loved the sound of that.

Selena pulled up to the curb of the two-story Mediterranean-style home with cream-colored stucco and a red tile roof in one of the newer multimillion dollar housing developments in San Bruno. It was a neighborhood that featured tiny, manicured yards and driveways filled with Teslas and BMWs.

She turned to Martina in the passenger seat and nodded. Selena turned off the engine and exited the vehicle. The air was chilly and smelled of fresh-cut grass.

The two women strutted up the walk to the front door. Butterflies roamed around Selena's belly as she knocked three times on the solid wood door. She was excited, but nervous too. It would be the first time she would interview clients and she wanted it to go well. She was aiming for a professional and mature vibe. It wasn't an easy look to pull off considering she was five foot three inches tall and only three months from her twentieth birthday. And no, she'd never been told she looked older. To her dismay, she'd often been mistaken for a high schooler instead of the college student that she was. Older folks often explained how great it was to appear younger than your years. They said she'd be grateful when she was older. She wondered when she'd be old enough for that to kick in. Selena glanced over at Martina, who was reading on her smartphone. *You can do this, Selena.*

A minute later, the door opened and a man with gray trousers, a white button-down shirt, and a dark five o'clock shadow stood with a long face. "Mr. Harrington?" Selena asked.

His face relaxed a bit. "Yes, you must be Selena and Martina."

Selena nodded. "Yes, I'm Selena Bailey," she said and extended her hand.

They shook and Mr. Harrington gave a nod. "Please call me Rick."

Martina tucked her phone in her shoulder bag. "And I'm Martina Monroe, we spoke on the phone. Pleasure to meet you." Mr. Harrington and Martina shook hands.

Mr. Harrington stepped back. "Please, come in."

Selena and Martina wiped their feet on the mat before entering the home. They were led into the first sitting room on the right. It was modern with two gray, contemporary sofas with brightly colored throw pillows facing one another in front of a fireplace with a marble mantel displaying family photos.

On one of the sofas, a woman in her thirties sat bouncing a small infant in her arms. Mr. Harrington stopped at the end of the sofa. "This is my wife, Julie, and the little one is Gemma. Julie, this is Selena Bailey and Martina Monroe."

Julie looked as if she were about to stand. Martina said, "Oh, please don't get up," and walked over to shake her one free hand. Selena repeated the gesture before taking a seat on the couch across from Julie, the baby, and now Rick.

Rick was middle-aged with salt-and-pepper hair, a contrast to the youthful wife beside him. She had to be at least ten years younger. Both had darker features and olive skin. Neither resem-

7

bled the photo of Emily sent in her email. Emily had cherubic features with wide blue eyes and a fair complexion.

Selena gave a reassuring smile. "Do you mind if we go ahead and get started?"

Rick said, "Yes, please do," while Julie unwrapped the baby's fingers from her long, dark hair and then nodded.

Selena straightened her posture. "I've read through the notes from the intake. It sounds like Julie, you were with Emily when she disappeared, three weeks ago Saturday. Can you tell me exactly what happened that day that you went to the nail salon, starting with leaving the home up until the point where Emily had disappeared?"

Julie let out a breath. "It was chaotic at home. Gemma was screaming. Emily was getting frustrated because she thought we would be late for our appointments. Emily likes to be on time. Finally, Rick took the baby and some formula and ushered us off so that we wouldn't miss our bonding time. We drove the ten minutes down to the salon and checked in for our appointments. The man at the desk brought us over to two pedicure chairs. Emily was sitting at the one on the end and I was next to her. Things seemed normal. And then I needed to use the bathroom. I assumed Emily would be fine for a few moments. So I quickly went to the restroom. I went and then came back out. I couldn't have been gone more than three minutes. She wasn't in the chair. I asked the nail technician about Emily. The woman just shook her head at me and didn't say anything. And then I said it louder. 'Where is Emily?' She just kept shaking her head back and forth while she drained the water from the foot soak Emily had used. So I went to the man at the front desk and asked about Emily. He said that he didn't know what I was talking about and that there was no little girl. I kind of lost it and started screaming at him. He told me I was crazy and should see a doctor."

Selena lifted her hand as if to stop her. "So the woman told you no, she hadn't seen Emily, even though she was actively cleaning up the spot where Emily had been sitting?"

Julie nodded emphatically. "Yes."

Selena cocked her head. "The man told you he never saw Emily with you?"

"Basically. He said, 'I don't know what you're talking about' and that he didn't see me arrive with a girl. He checked us in! I demanded to know where she went. He said that I was crazy and that I should go and find a doctor before I hurt myself. He told me not to pay, to just go. So, I ran out of the of the salon and checked the parking lot for any sign of her. When I couldn't find her, I called the police on my phone."

Julie's voice was beginning to shake. Selena didn't think it was because she was nervous. It seemed more like she was genuinely traumatized by the experience and distraught over the disappearance of her daughter. "How long did it take for the police to arrive?"

"God, it seemed like forever, at least ten minutes."

"Ten minutes?"

"Yes, it took so long. It felt like forever as I stood out there by myself. I called Rick and told him what had happened. At first he didn't understand because the baby was screaming and I just ..." Julie's gaze stared out at the family photo and tears streamed down her cheeks.

Selena wondered if the woman blamed herself for losing Emily or if she was simply putting on a great show. "Had you been to the nail salon before?" Selena asked.

Julie wiped her face with the back of her hand. "No. I found them on Yelp. They were the only one who had available appointments. It was kind of a last-minute plan. But I know something strange is going on there. The way that they insisted they hadn't seen her, it wasn't right. It was as if it was

9

rehearsed. For them to deny she'd been there, they had to have taken her."

Rick wrapped his arm around Julie's shoulders in what looked like an attempt to console her.

Selena glanced at Martina, who gave her an encouraging nod to continue. "Is there anything else you can tell me about that day? Did you notice anyone who seemed suspicious or out of place, either in the neighborhood or around the nail salon?"

Julie shook her head. "No."

"Maybe a new face around the neighborhood or Emily's school in the days or weeks leading up to her disappearance?"

Julie looked up as if trying to recall. She shook her head. "No."

If that were true, it was likely Emily either disappeared at the nail salon or at the hands of her parents. Selena set down her notebook. "I noticed that neither of you resemble Emily physically. Was she adopted?"

Rick was about to speak when the infant in his wife's arms began to wail. Julie stood up from the couch, baby in her arms, and began to bounce her. She looked over at Selena. "I'm sorry. I think she may be ready for her feeding. Rick, you go ahead. I'll be back as soon as I can." She exited the living room and went upstairs, presumably to a nursery.

Selena said, "You were saying?"

His face fell. "No, Emily was not adopted. She's my daughter from a previous marriage. Unfortunately, her mother passed away recently and Emily came to live with us full-time seven months ago when her mother was too sick to care for her. It was so great to have Emily around ..." Before he could finish his thoughts, he closed his eyes and bowed his head, placing them into his hands. His body shook.

Martina dug into her purse and pulled out a packet of tissues. She got up from the couch and placed them next to him on the sofa. He looked up at her with sad, watery eyes. "Thank you." He grabbed a tissue out of the plastic package and dabbed his eyes. "Her mother moved to Oregon shortly after we split up five years ago, so I only saw Emily when I flew up there or when she came here for the summer. Her mother was diagnosed with cancer a year and a half ago, and when she became too sick to take care of Emily, we had Emily come live with us. She got her looks from her mother."

Seven months ago? When they were already expecting a new baby? How did Julie Harrington feel about that?

"How did Emily adjust to being here with you and your wife and the new baby?"

"It was hard at first. She missed her mother terribly. Gemma was born six weeks ago. That's been a new challenge as well. Sometimes I think I'm just too old for this. But Julie's been so great. She wanted to bond with Emily and be a mother for her. It's why they went to the salon that day, to have some bonding time without the baby and me."

Difficult child. A stepmother with a newborn. She could see why the investigation from the police department had shifted to the family. The father was certainly stricken by Emily's disappearance, and Julie too. But was it all an act? "I'm so sorry this is happening, Rick. We're going to do everything we can to find Emily. Do you mind if I look around a little bit? I'd also like to see her room, if that's okay."

"Yes, that's fine."

Selena stood up and eased over to the fireplace mantel. There were family photos of Rick, Julie, Emily, and the new baby. And more photos of the new baby. *And more photos of the baby.* She turned around to Rick. "Did Emily have a school photo taken this year?"

"Yes, they're around here somewhere. I think we just got the packet back recently."

School photos not up in the house. Too busy with the new baby? Or too busy dealing with a difficult seven-year-old? Or did they know she wouldn't be around, so what's the point? "And her room is upstairs?" Selena asked.

"Yes, let me show you." Rick pushed off of the sofa and led Selena and Martina up the tall staircase. At the top of the stairs he pointed to the left. "That's Emily's room. I have a hard time going in there. We haven't touched it since the police were here."

Selena and Martina entered silently. The room had a large window above a red play tee-pee next to a bookshelf that had books half pushed out and some on the floor. On the far wall was a white dresser with drawers open and clothing spilling out. A twin bed was stripped of any coverings. The walls were adorned with posters of colorful birds. Selena walked over to the closet. Coats, shoes, and dresses were shoved aside as if someone had been searching for clues. Selena picked up a red plaid dress from the bottom of the closet and rehung it on a hanger. From behind she heard, "That was her favorite."

Selena turned around to see Julie standing in the doorway. Rick was behind her. "Is that right?" Selena asked.

"Yes, we bought it for her to wear to the Nutcracker Ballet at Christmas time. Red is her favorite color."

"And she likes birds?"

Julie's eyes widened and a small smile formed on her face. "Oh, yes. She *loves* birds. *Loves*. Talks about them nonstop. Actually, it's sweet, she calls Gemma, baby bird." Tears returned to Julie's eyes.

Selena looked at the floor as Julie composed herself. The ground was covered in books, dolls, and clothes. "Was Emily a messy child?"

Julie wiped the corner of her eyes. "Oh no. She was fastidiously neat. The police did this. She'd have a meltdown if she saw what they did."

Emily was a neat child who loved birds. And had meltdowns.

"Can we get a tour of the rest of the home?"

Julie answered, "Of course, but please, keep quiet if you can. I just put Gemma down."

Martina whispered, "No problem. I understand. My baby is now twenty-one, but I remember those days and nights like they were yesterday."

Selena wondered what it was like for Zoey, Martina's daughter, growing up with Martina from day one. It was probably pretty great.

At the end of the tour, after nothing seemed abnormal or out of place, Selena said, "We can see ourselves out. We'll be in touch as we have more information."

Rick eyed both Selena and Martina. "Thank you, thank you both. We just want her to come home. That's all we want."

As they waved goodbye, Rick stood in the hall with his arm around Julie's shoulders.

Selena thought the Harringtons' grief seemed genuine. But so did so many other child killers who paraded in front of the news channels begging for the public to help them find their children, only to find out later they had in fact murdered their own flesh and blood. Were the Harringtons genuine or did they deserve an Oscar for their performance?

3

The next morning, Selena woke up nestled under the covers in Brendon's bed. It was officially the weekend. No classes to attend, but she did have an important mission that day. Today was the day she went on her first undercover mission at the nail salon. She was more nervous than she'd expected and had tossed and turned most of the night. Martina had assured her that she'd done great with the Harringtons, but it was one thing to interview clients, quite another to try to gather intel from possible hostiles.

Selena realized she should be counting her lucky stars she was even able to work the investigation, which was even more pressure to do the job well.

Martina was more than a little upset a year ago when Selena had launched her own investigation and surveillance of the Delta Kappa Alpha fraternity house after Dee had been attacked at one of their parties. The police tasked with prosecuting the assault had failed to do so, claiming it was just another case of "he said, she said," but Selena knew something bigger was going on, so she'd taken matters into her own hands. Of course, the operation hadn't gone exactly to plan, but with the help of

Martina, the fraternity lost their charter and one bad guy was arrested and later prosecuted, since the attack had been captured on video.

Selena had done some questionable and dangerous things that Martina wasn't very happy about. She essentially had no backup and nobody knew what she was up to other than Dee, who had already gone home to Sacramento when the shit hit the fan. After oodles of lectures by Martina and her dad, Selena promised not to do any more unsanctioned undercover or investigative work.

She glanced over at Brendon, still sleeping soundly. She had been so lucky to meet him. He wasn't just easy on the eyes, he made her laugh like nobody had ever made her laugh before.

Brendon was a political science major who wanted to become a lawyer and then enter politics to try to reform the justice system. She kissed him lightly on the cheek and whispered in his ear. "I have to go. I'll call you later, okay?"

He grumbled a protest before turning onto his side, scooping her up with his right arm. "No, don't go. Do you have to?"

She ran her fingers through his light brown hair. "You know today's my first undercover assignment."

He opened his eyes and stared into hers. "That's right. Good luck. Call me later and tell me how it goes, okay?"

She gave him a quick peck on the lips before sliding off the bed. "All right. Call you later." She pulled on her jeans and sweater and grabbed her coat before hurrying down the hall and out of his apartment. Locking the door behind her, she hopped down the stairs to the street as the cold February wind blasted her in the face. She rushed over to her car, which was parked directly in front of the building. She entered the driver's side and turned on the car. She rubbed her hands together before she turned on the radio. Then she turned up the volume and drove toward home to pick up Dee for their mission.

After showering and eating a healthy breakfast of broccoli and egg scramble, Dee and Selena headed toward the nail salon in the town of San Bruno. During the twenty-five minute drive, Selena prepped Dee, who had enthusiastically agreed to a free manicure and pedicure as payment for being Selena's undercover sidekick as well as providing a full download of her observations back at the offices of Drakos Monroe. Selena explained. "Take notice of anything unusual or unusual for a nail salon. Items that aren't typically there or odd conversations."

Dee continued to focus on applying lip gloss in the visor mirror. "Got it. Oh, and if you need me to assist in any other stakeouts where you need me to get a massage or a facial or anything like that, I'm happy to help."

Selena cracked a grin. It was nice to have company on her first stakeout. She'd convinced Martina it would be less conspicuous to have the two of them getting mani-pedis. Martina had agreed to the expenditure almost immediately. It was a win-win.

They approached the strip mall and took notice of the nearly full parking lot. Selena found a spot several yards away from Pretty Nails, the nail salon in question.

As they approached the storefront made of glass, Selena was surprised to find it nearly full. Odd for February. Nobody was wearing flip-flops or open-toed shoes in the frigid San Francisco Bay Area air. She pushed open the glass door of the salon and the set of bells hanging on the handle jingled, notifying the establishment they'd arrived.

Selena approached a middle-aged man with dark hair and weathered skin. She thought, *Not sure I've seen a man working at a nail salon before.* Maybe he was the owner? He gave what appeared to be a forced smiled and a set of crooked teeth greeted her. "How may I help you?"

Selena brightened her expression. "Hi, my name is Selena Jones and this is my friend, Dee Smith. We both have appointments for manicures and pedicures." Selena had originally considered fake first and last names, but she was concerned her and Dee may slip up and say their first names so she'd opted for only false last names.

The man studied the computer monitor and then glanced back up at Selena. "Oh yes, right here. Please come this way."

Selena glanced over at Dee and then followed the man over to the first row of pedicure chairs, each equipped with its own foot basin at the bottom. The man pointed. "You here and you here." He turned around and said something in another language to two women who then scurried over to Dee and Selena's chairs.

Selena sat back into the leather chair. *Not too shabby*. She glanced up. The nail salon had a front desk outlined with UV light kiosks for drying nails, and then six pedicure chairs on each side of the room. It was decorated with tacky posters of brightly colored fingernails. Next to the last chair on the end was a small poster advertising mother-daughter specials. *Interesting*. At the end of the row of chairs was a back room, presumably where the restroom and storage closets were located. Across the room, she saw other women reading on electronic devices, magazines, or chatting with the person next to them. All chairs were full.

Selena glanced down at the woman who was now filling up the water basin with hot water and pouring a blue powder into the pool. She couldn't be much older than herself. The woman looked up at Selena with red-rimmed eyes. "How the tempature?"

Selena smiled. "It's great. Oh, I like your nails."

The woman gave a pursed grin and a head nod.

The woman's neon orange fingernails and toenails were a

stark contrast to her relatively drab attire of black cotton pants and a faded green t-shirt.

She turned to Dee, who was leaned back in the chair with her eyes closed and her hand on the massage function controller. "Enjoying yourself?" Selena asked.

Dee's aqua blue eyes popped open. "Yes, I could definitely get used to this."

"Me too."

Selena looked down again at her technician. "So you get a lot of mothers and daughters in here for your special? I was thinking maybe I should bring my mom."

Lie. Her mother was dead, killed by her scumbag boyfriend who was now serving a life sentence at San Quentin.

The woman gave her the same tight smile and nod. Selena wondered how much English the women knew. Selena leaned forward and asked Dee's technician, an older woman with graying hair and dark eyes, "Do you speak English?"

"Little English."

Selena continued her line of questioning. "Do you get a lot of mothers and their young daughters? Or mostly adults?"

She smiled and nodded, revealing a missing incisor. "Mothers and daughters."

She did warn her *little English*.

In the hour she sat in the chair, both men and women came and went. Progressive men getting pedis? Businessmen? She couldn't imagine Brendon or her father ever stepping foot in a nail salon let alone sitting there long enough for a mani-pedi. Business was booming. Surprising, considering supposedly a little girl had gone missing from the salon three weeks ago. Even if it hadn't been proven, it seemed as though it would have dampened business a little.

The technician slipped Selena's flip-flops on after painting her toenails. Selena wiggled her glittery blue toenails. "I love them. Thank you. Is there a bathroom I can use?"

The woman pointed down the hall.

Selena gave her best warm smile and climbed off of the chair. She gave Dee the cash to pay before casually strolling down the row of pedicure chairs toward the back room. She entered the dark hall and saw the restroom labeled with a brass plaque on the right. To the left were two more shut, unlabeled doors. She glanced back over her shoulder at the salon. Nobody had eyes on her.

She opened the first door on the left and peered inside. It looked like mostly supplies, wax, towels, cotton tow separators, and other assorted items you'd expect at a nail salon. She glanced over her shoulder again. Still, nobody paid any attention to her snooping. She looked at the door straight ahead and twisted the knob. She was surprised to open the door and find more doors. The place was like a freaking maze. *Odd.*

She opened the first one on the left and stepped back. Her mouth dropped open. There were five mattresses on the floor with little piles of clothes and shoes near each one. The women were sleeping there? *This can't be legal.* She pulled out her phone and snapped a picture before softly closing the door.

She opened the next door and froze at the of the sight of the half-dressed man behind the door. She glanced to her left and eyed a young woman cowering under a sheet atop a queen-size bed. The man pushed Selena back and shut the door in her face.

Selena spun around to exit as quickly as possible. She didn't want to be discovered poking around. She rushed to the front of the salon where Dee sat with her hands under UV lamps that emitted a purple glow. She bent down and whispered in her ear. "We have to go. *Now.*"

4

Selena ran out to her car and jumped into the driver's seat. She waited for Dee to catch up and they sped off. On the road toward Drakos Monroe Security and Investigations, Selena described what she witnessed to Dee. Dee's eyes widened and her mouth dropped open. "Oh my god. Yes. That totally fits. Those women are being trafficked."

Selena shook her head while keeping her eyes on the road. "What do you mean?"

"Nail salons are notorious for human trafficking. I was watching and observing the women. All of the red flags are there. The only one who can speak fluent English is the man at the counter and he watches each of them rather closely. None of them seem particularly well-dressed and none maintained eye contact. And the fact that there are mattresses means those women are likely living there. All classic signs of them being trafficked. Sometimes what happens is they are brought to the United States under false promises that they'll be working and making money to send home. But in reality, they're trapped into modern-day slavery. I bet those women aren't paid or even fed very well. And the fact there was a man that was half-dressed with another woman underneath the sheet—maybe they're being forced into the sex trade as well. Are we gonna shut them down?"

Selena tried her hardest to focus on the road. But she couldn't believe what she was hearing. How had the police not discovered this during their search for Emily?

"How do you know this? And if they're trafficking young Asian women, how would blond-haired, blue-eyed Emily fit in?"

"At the center, they train us to look for the signs. One reason is to help the women who come into the center and to be on the lookout in our everyday lives. As for how Emily fits in? I don't know, but trafficking is organized crime. As soon as the little girl's mother complained her child was gone, they probably used bleach to clean up every surface. Also, they probably hid all of the women's belongings when the police searched. You said that it was basically just plain mattresses on the floor? They probably have a quick way of turning it over to look more normal. These types of operations have dozens of people in on the crime. They may even have a crew just for the purpose of a quick cover-up."

Selena twisted her face in disgust. "I can't believe that stuff happens here." How could there be human trafficking in the San Francisco Bay Area? She thought that kind of thing only happened overseas, in corrupt countries.

Dee sighed. "It happens everywhere."

That is truly horrifying. And what about Emily Harrington? Was her disappearance connected to a human trafficking ring?

They arrived at Drakos Monroe and were greeted warmly by the receptionist, Mrs. Pearson, who was wearing her signature bright pink lipstick and carefully coiffed hair. After introductions, Dee and Selena strolled past and into the cubicle area, where they found Martina chatting with another member of the team. Martina seemed relieved at the sight of them back safe and sound. She waved. "Let's meet in conference room two, in five minutes, okay?"

"Sure."

Dee and Selena headed down the hall and entered the small conference room that had whiteboard paint on the walls, a table, and four chairs. Dee swirled around in the chair and her golden hair swung across her face. "This place is so cool. You think I could get a gig here?"

"Probably. You could ask Martina when she arrives. I didn't realize you were interested in this type of work."

Dee tucked a strand of hair behind her ear. "I don't know about that, I still have my sights on medical school, but it could be interesting. And I can always use a little extra cash."

"I can ask her for you." Selena glanced up. "Oh, hi, Martina."

Martina ran her fingers through her short, dark hair before taking a seat. "Hello, ladies. I'm glad to see you back. How did it go at the nail salon?"

Had Martina been concerned? It wasn't exactly the most high-stakes undercover operation. Although someone did catch her sneaking around. If they remembered her, that could be bad. *Very bad.*

Selena sat up straight in the chair and gave Martina the full lowdown on what had happened.

Martina's face melted. "They caught you snooping around?"

"One guy. It wasn't the guy who was at the front desk."

After hearing herself say the words, she realized it sounded stupid. If they had cameras back there, they would have her on film poking around. She of course could easily explain her presence in the back room by simply saying she was just looking for the bathroom. *As one always does when caught sneaking around.*

Martina eyed the two of them and then focused on Selena. "It goes without saying that that neither one of you can go back into that nail salon, ever. Are we clear?"

Selena nodded.

Dee held up her hand. "Fine by me. They didn't do a very good job anyways. Look at that. She painted my cuticle on two different fingers."

Selena restrained a chuckle.

Martina's face remained serious. "Thank you for going along, Dee. It's appreciated, you made good observations."

"No problem. Glad I could help. Hopefully you'll find Emily. But what do you plan to do about the human trafficking? Are you going to tell the police? They need to be shut down. I read an article last week that said that human trafficking was on the rise and that it's the fastest growing business in the United States right now."

Martina shut her eyes and shook her head. "I know. It's horrible. But, I'm not sure we should notify the police quite yet. If the salon is somehow connected to Emily's disappearance, it would be better for us to keep a close eye, but not to spook them. If they pack up and leave, we may never find Emily."

Selena's instincts were telling her that the alleged trafficking ring was in fact connected to Emily Harrington, but how? She said, "Okay, I hear you about the human trafficking, but it doesn't really seem to fit that they would steal a seven-year-old girl with blonde hair and blue eyes, right? All those women didn't speak English and were clearly from another country. It seems a very different model than kidnapping children who come into the nail salon, right?"

Martina tipped her head. "Organized crime isn't usually limited to just one line of business. If they're caught up in the sex trade, chances are someone like Emily—as awful as it sounds—could have been a special order. You said there were signs advertising mother-daughter specials? It could be that is how they're luring girls in. And maybe it only earned them one girl, but, frankly, someone like Emily could be worth a lot on the black market."

Selena stomach soured. The thought disgusted her. Why were there so many monsters in the world? More importantly, how could she stop them? "I don't get how the police didn't find anything when they searched."

Martina provided a similar explanation as Dee. "It's a nail salon. It's easily cleaned up with a little bleach. It is also a possibility that—" Martina paused. "I'm sorry, it's your case. What do you think the other possibilities are?"

Selena met Martina's stern gaze. "She was never there."

"Exactly," Martina agreed.

"You met the parents. What's your take?" Selena asked.

"I could go either way right now. They seem sincere, but you never know. We need to follow the evidence, and right now we don't really have any." Martina turned to Dee, who was watching them intently, before returning to Selena. "I was thinking we talk next steps, but I don't want to bore Dee. Did you drive separate?"

"No, I drove us both here."

Martina picked up her phone. "No problem, I'll have one of my staff give Dee a lift back."

Selena thought, *Damn. Martina was bad ass. 'I'll just have my staff give you a lift.' 100% Girl Boss.*

Martina eyed Dee. "Is that okay with you?"

"Yeah, great. Thank you."

"Go ahead and tell Mrs. Pearson I okay'd it. She'll know what to do. Thank you again for your help, Dee."

"No problem. See ya back at the house, Selena."

Dee scooted out of her chair and headed toward the door.

Selena waved before Dee disappeared into the hall.

At the end of their two-hour strategy session, Martina said, "Okay. We sit tight until the background comes back on the nail salon and owner. That should work perfectly to give you some time this weekend to do homework and have some fun. I'll let you know as soon as the intel comes in."

Selena didn't like the idea of sitting tight. She wanted to be doing. She wanted to find out what happened to Emily. "Are you sure there's nothing we can do?"

Martina shook her head. "No, it's far too dangerous to initiate a stakeout until we know who we're dealing with. If they are traffickers, we may need to reevaluate our strategy. Until then, we'll have Team One begin surveillance on the Harringtons."

A mixture of excitement and nerves formed in her stomach. It had become clear that although they were being paid by the family, they also needed to investigate the family. The more they knew about Emily's life, the more likely they'd be able to find out what happened to her and hopefully find her safe and sound. *Fingers crossed.*

5

Selena chewed a mouthful of Ceasar salad while admiring Brendon's childlike excitement.

"Can you believe it? I'm going to intern this summer at the mayor's office. I can't wait. Not only will I learn a ton, but it will look great on my law school applications."

She swallowed and smiled at him. "I'm so happy for you. And boy, are you a think-ahead type. Law school applications aren't for another two or three years, right?"

He nodded. "Yes, I won't apply until I take the LSAT senior year. I have two more years, but now is the time to start building my resume. Getting into a top law school is pretty important for what I want to do."

Selena admired his drive and ambition. She sometimes couldn't believe she was dating a future politician. It was so different than what she imagined for her own life. All she ever wanted was to not have to worry about how she'd pay the bills and to help others. Brendon's mission wasn't much different. Although he hadn't grown up wondering whether or not they'd make rent, he also wanted to help others, but in a much more public way. Selena couldn't imagine a life in the spotlight. Yet, they seemed to fit ... for now. It was something she worried about from time to time, but she mostly tried to enjoy the here and now. Life was made for living.

"Well, I'm happy for you. I'm sure you'll be a star intern."

He beamed at her. "I don't know about star. Speaking of, how is the case going and the stakeout? I want to hear everything!"

Selena wiped her fingers on the paper napkin and told him the details of her interview with the Harringtons and the under-cover operation. After her synopsis, she explained, "I can't wait to dig deeper. There is something really off about this case. I think if I can get a better look at the nail salon, I can put the pieces of the puzzle together. But, I'm on strict orders from Martina to stay away from the salon until our analysts can pull the background information on the owner and business histo-ry." She grabbed her plastic cup full of water and took a sip. She glanced across at Brendon. There was no encouraging smile and his fair complexion had gone ashen. "What's wrong?" Selena asked.

His eyes widened. "Trafficking? That's organized crime. Those type of groups have been known to be extremely violent if provoked. I ... I'm worried about you. I had no idea a private investigator's job would be so dangerous. I thought you'd be chasing down cheating husbands or something."

Why would he think she'd possibly want a career chasing down cheating husbands? She suddenly lost her appetite and pushed her plate away. "This is the job. And no, it's not always so dangerous, but it can be. Drakos Monroe is security and investi-gations, which means we take some of the more high-risk cases like missing persons and persons who need protecting. Sure, the bread-and-butter work is less sexy, like background checks, insurance fraud, and digging up info for lawsuits. But what I love is the investigations. Trying to put all the clues together. It's fascinating."

He shook his head. "I'm sorry, I didn't realize that. Wow. I see why you'd want to do that, I guess."

He guessed? "What do you mean? You've known I would either go into law enforcement or private investigations at my stepmom's firm. I told you I wanted to help people, like how my stepmom and Detective Gates helped to save me. That's the kind of job I want." Her body shook at the memory of Detective Gates kicking down the door, shooting her attacker, then creepy boyfriend, Zeek, and then being rushed to safety by Martina. Two years later and the flashbacks still rocked her.

His body relaxed. "You're right. I'm sorry. I guess I just like to think of you *not* being in danger. I know you're tough and can handle yourself. I just can't imagine losing you. It feels different hearing the details. I guess since you haven't been in the field much it didn't really sink in until now, that's all. I'm sure I'll get used to it. If you're happy, I'm happy."

"I am happy. I love the fact that I may be able to save a little girl when traditional law enforcement couldn't."

He cocked his head. "That's amazing, sweetheart. Forgive me?"

She gave him a lopsided grin. "I guess."

"I'll take it. Now what do you say we get outta here and go to the movies?"

She grinned. "Let's do it." Despite her smiles, Selena still felt a bit off-kilter about the conversation. She wondered how supportive Brendon would be when she was a PI or detective full-time and tracking down bad guys on a regular basis? This was just day one. She shook it off and opted for having a fun night filled with movie theater popcorn, sugary snacks, and Brendon's warm body next to hers.

Selena typed the last sentence of the essay due the next day for her Criminal Theory class. She couldn't believe she was at home working on homework instead of going out investigating the disappearance of Emily Harrington. But strict orders from Martina made sure she wouldn't be near the nail salon again. Selena began to wonder, what was the point of getting her degree in criminal justice anyway? She didn't need a college degree to become a private investigator or a detective, and as long as she kept getting her hours through Drakos Monroe she would be eligible to receive her license in the next year. As if answering her question, her telephone buzzed on top of her desk. She picked it up. "Hey, Martina."

"Hi, how is it going?"

"Great, I just finished the last of my homework for tomorrow. What's up, did you find something new in the case?"

"I was able to set up an interview with the lead detective at the San Bruno Police Department so that you can interview him about the case. I wasn't able to get a hold of anybody at Emily's school, so I'll have one of my staff go ahead and give Emily's school a call tomorrow and try to set up some time with Emily's teacher."

Thank god. She couldn't wait to get back on the case. Compared to the investigation, her classes were like watching paint dry.

Selena slipped out of her desk chair and climbed on to her bed. "Great. You think the detective will be forthcoming about the case?"

"I hope so. I had to pull a few favors to get you the interview."

The benefits of being a badass like Martina seemed to be

endless. "I suppose there isn't anything else I can do until tomorrow then?"

"You have your interview questions prepared, right?"

"Yep." She created the list of questions for the police and Emily's teacher nearly immediately after leaving the Harringtons' residence on Friday evening. She was ready to interview and continue working on the case. She was dying to stakeout the nail salon at night, presumably when there would be a lot of activity, if they were in fact prostituting the women. But she was on orders to stand down. If she just happened to drive by one night, it wouldn't be considered a stakeout, right?

"Great. I'll have my assistant send you the details for the detective interview. One more thing, I was planning to call Dee tomorrow, but if we can get her in the office this week, we can have her submit a formal application, and get the paperwork completed to get her on payroll. If she acts fast, she can assist you on the case. I figure she could be setting up appointments, reviewing records, and that sort of thing. Do you think you'll have the bandwidth to train Dee on those activities?"

Selena was being pulled pretty thin, but she was confident that she could handle school, lead an investigation, and date Brendon. Sure, she'd had a lot more late nights than before, but she could do it. If she had to stretch herself a little thinner to train Dee so that she could give Dee the grunt work, so be it. "Yes, not a problem. She should be home soon, I'll tell her the news."

"Great. I'll give her a call tomorrow too and give her the official word and then you two can set up some time to go over the training and how everything works."

"Sounds like a plan."

"Give me a call before you head to the police station, okay?"

Of course. Selena had been instructed to check in every single step of the way. "Will do."

Selena hung up the phone. She definitely liked the idea of pushing off the tedious work to somebody else. She didn't think Dee would mind too much. Dee loved numbers and all things analytical. It would probably be a welcome break from her more challenging science classes. Plus, as Selena learned, in this business everybody had to start at the bottom. *Wasn't that the truth.*

6

As the rain poured down, Selena hurried toward the main office of Sweeney Ridge Elementary School. When she reached the door, she tussled her now damp long, wavy locks. Having forgotten her umbrella at home, she was now wet from head to toe. She removed her coat and shook it out before she pulled open the door in an attempt to avoid creating a puddle inside of the school.

She'd been thrilled when she'd received the call first thing Monday morning and learned that Emily's second grade teacher had been available for an interview. She liked the idea of getting details about Emily from her teacher before heading over to the police station that afternoon. With an exasperated smile, she approached the desk adorned with red and pink heart doilies. She glanced around the office. The walls were decorated with cardboard hearts and cupids. *Right. Valentine's Day is coming soon.* Behind the desk sat a woman with wire-rimmed glasses and a furrowed brow. "May I help you?"

"Yes, my name is Selena Bailey and I'm here to see Mrs. Anderson. We have an appointment."

"Oh yes, of course. Why don't you have a seat over there. I'll call her classroom. She should be up shortly."

Selena took a seat across from the receptionist who was the only other person inside the office. Not surprising considering it was four-thirty in the afternoon, school had been out for almost two hours. Most teachers had probably gone home along with the nurse and other administrative staff.

Selena reread her notes on Mrs. Anderson, Emily's second grade teacher. She'd been teaching for over twenty years, but had only known Emily since the fall when she'd come to live with Rick and Julie Harrington. Selena wondered what she would learn from the teacher. Was Emily a good student who paid attention in class and achieved good grades? Did she have many friends? A chill shot through her. She could only imagine where Emily was right now.

The poor girl. First she'd lost her mother and had been forced to move to a new city and school, and now she was kidnapped or dead or worse. The most vile monsters were the ones who took children and sold them like they were commodities. It was too awful to contemplate. Her stomach churned at the thoughts and she was now regretting the green smoothie she had drank before the meeting. It was *not* sitting right with her.

The door to the office creaked open and footsteps drew near. Selena glanced up. The petite woman with ebony skin and hair pulled tight in a bun gave a warm smile. "Are you Selena Bailey?"

Selena stood up and extended her hand. "Yes, you must be Mrs. Anderson?"

"Yes, I am. Why don't you come back with me to my classroom and we can discuss Emily. Do you not have an umbrella?"

Selena gave a sheepish look. "No."

"Well, you can share with me. It's not far."

"Thank you." Selena followed Mrs. Anderson out of the office. Mrs. Anderson picked up her umbrella from the ground and lifted it. "C'mon now."

Selena huddled next to the teacher and tried to keep up. The woman moved quite quickly for as tiny as she was. When they reached the classroom, Mrs. Anderson held the door open as Selena scrambled inside.

The classroom walls were colorful with children's art projects with an obvious Valentine theme as well as calendars and multiplication tables. Selena followed past the thirty or so student desks to the front of the classroom, where Mrs. Anderson's solid wood desk resided. Mrs. Anderson sat behind her desk and gestured for Selena to take the child-sized chair next to her.

"So, Ms. Bailey, what can I answer about Emily? Terrible that she's gone missing."

"I was hired by the family to look into her disappearance, since the police have run out of leads. We're starting from the beginning and trying to learn as much about Emily's life as we can. I wanted to talk to you specifically about Emily and how she acted in class, if she had many friends, how she performed in school, and your overall impression of the girl."

Mrs. Anderson sat back in her chair and folded her arms. "That girl. She didn't like to sit still. And she didn't like to hand in her homework. I don't think she has many friends. She is kind of shy. But oh, how she loves birds."

Selena jotted down. *Really Loves Birds. Not many friends. Didn't do homework.* "So if she wasn't turning in her homework, did you have a parent-teacher conference with her father and stepmother to understand why?"

Mrs. Anderson sighed. "I tried to get them down here, but the only conversations I could have with her father were over the phone. I think they're having a bit of an adjustment since Emily came to live with them. When I explained to Mr. Harrington that she wasn't turning in her homework and that I was concerned, he said that he would have a talk with her."

Selena took more notes on her notepad. *Father not coming to the school to talk with the teacher—only on the phone.*

"You said she couldn't sit still. Can you describe that more for me?"

"Well, if it were up to her, she'd stand over at the window all day. She didn't like to stay in her seat." Mrs. Anderson pointed. "She said she was watching the birds. She was a bit withdrawn. Not unusual, considering she just lost her mother. But I had to explain to her that she had to sit down in the classroom because those were the rules."

"Did she eventually sit down in her chair?"

"Eventually. But there were some days I had to keep on with the class while she stood and stared out the window. Otherwise, the other children would miss their lesson and that's not fair to them."

"I'm assuming that warranted another call home to her parents?"

"Yes. Again, Mr. Harrington said he would speak with Emily."

"After you spoke with him, did it improve? Did she remain seated?"

Mrs. Anderson's face turned downward. "Not really. I think what she needed was to have a little more time to adjust to living in a new home with new parents, new school, and not having her mother anymore. Unfortunately, there was more than one occasion when I had to send her to the office because she was disrupting the other students."

"How so?"

"When she was sitting in her chair, she liked to tap her pencil on the desk or make other sort of ruckus. She dropped books on the ground. All seemed to be attention-seeking activities. I thought maybe she should see a counselor. I again called her home and suggested it."

It seemed like Mrs. Anderson communicated with the parents quite a bit, but reading between the lines, the parents didn't seem to have done anything about Emily's behavioral issues. Was Emily a problem child? Had she gotten to be too much for them to handle, especially once the new baby came along? "Did Emily see a counselor?" Selena asked.

"Not that I'm aware of. Unfortunately, I had called them the week before Emily disappeared. I haven't spoken with them since. My heart breaks for that girl. I hope you find her and bring her home and hopefully get her some help."

Interesting. Was it possible that Emily really had never been at the nail salon and that Julie and Rick Harrington used it as a cover for what they had done to her? Maybe Emily was accidentally killed? An accidental fall or shove down the stairs? The Harringtons' grief seemed genuine. Perhaps it was, and they were now remorseful?

"Well, thank you very much for speaking with me today. You've been very helpful."

"Not a problem. Please let me know if you have any more questions. I'll be happy to answer them. Anything to help bring Emily home."

Selena took a business card from her purse and handed it to the teacher. "Thank you. Please call if you think of anything that could help us find Emily." She put her coat on and showed herself out of the portable classroom. She ran down the ramp and continued to the parking lot, into the shelter of her warm and dry car.

She started the engine and flicked on the windshield wipers.

She sat for a moment and contemplated what she'd just learned. It wouldn't be unheard of for a parent to lose control over a difficult child, especially one that had just moved in with them seven months ago and the added stresses of an infant. It would definitely be interesting to find out what the police had to say about that.

Selena sat across the table from Detective Faber of the San Bruno Police Department. The cramped conference room was stuffy and smelled of disinfectant. She wondered if it was a room used to interrogated suspects. After the usual pleasantries and introductions and basic questions, Selena asked, "When you went to the nail salon, did you find anything unusual?"

Detective Faber shrugged. "Not really."

Selena cocked her head. "No sign of anyone living there or perhaps they were being held against their will?"

The detective scratched the top of his shiny, bald head. "No, we didn't find any evidence of that. Not that, that isn't something that could be happening there, but we didn't find any evidence of it. There were no living quarters and none of the women said they were there unwillingly. Why do you ask?"

Selena had instructions not to tell the police about what she'd found at the nail salon, especially since she'd just been there. A raid shortly after she'd been spotted could lead the salon owners to associate the raid with Selena. Martina had warned that it was far too dangerous for her to report them yet.

Selena gave a tight-lipped grin. "Nothing in particular, other than the reputation of these nail salons for being sites of human trafficking. That and of course massage parlors. Quite disheartening that this sort of thing is happening in the Bay Area, isn't it?"

Detective Faber nodded. "Yes, it is. We have a task force assigned to look for signs and to bring down some of these trafficking rings that somehow think that the Bay Area is a great place for this type of activity. Unfortunately, the only reason they're here is because there is a demand for it. Especially the massage parlors."

Yes, especially the massage parlors. After Dee had explained to her about trafficking in the Bay Area, Selena went online for more information. What she found wasn't good news and it only reiterated what Dee had explained. It was happening everywhere, and not only to women being sold into the sex trade. Men, women, and children were being forced into modern-day slavery and being used at construction sites, restaurants, elder care centers, nail salons, agricultural fields, escort services, truck stops, and hotels all over the San Francisco Bay Area and throughout the United States. One article stated trafficking was the new crack cocaine. *How was this not headline news all day, every day?*

Selena sighed. "And you didn't find any trace of Emily at the nail salon or anywhere near it? Did you try traffic cams for any sighting of Emily around or near the salon?"

"Even if we had the manpower to check every traffic cam footage in the area, there aren't any close enough to the nail salon to prove she'd been there."

Selena noted the lack of cameras near the nail salon. Was it by design? "Why did you shift the investigation towards the family?"

"I can't discuss any evidence, especially since you were hired by the family, but what I can tell you is that they have the trifecta. Motive, means, and opportunity. The nail salon on the other hand, has no evidence she was ever there, let alone motive to take Emily. Unless of course, to your point, they're in the sex trade and good at covering it up."

"In the search by the police department and community, there was no sign of her living or not living?"

The detective shook his head. "It was as if she disappeared without a trace."

"Did you find it strange that the workers there said they had never seen Emily that day?" Selena asked.

"If she was there, it's very strange. But if she was never there, not strange at all."

Exactly. She hadn't gleaned much from the interview with the detective other than there was clearly no evidence pointing in any direction to what happened to Emily. How does a person go missing without a single clue?

Selena thanked the detective and exited the police station. It had stopped raining. *Thank god.* She walked to her car and slid onto the driver's seat. She lifted the key and had almost inserted it when she paused. She was already in San Bruno. It couldn't possibly hurt to drive past the nail salon, right?

She grabbed a baseball cap from her back seat and tugged it on. She slipped her sunglasses on and started the engine. It was a bit dark, but she could manage.

Ten minutes later, she approached the strip mall where the nail salon was located. Another packed parking lot. She drove into the lot and snaked around to the back of the building to a road usually designated for deliveries and employees of the shops within the strip mall. She drove slowly and paused at the back entrance of the nail salon. There was a single white door closed shut.

She glanced along the back wall and surrounding area. There didn't appear to be any type of cameras or surveillance, or any lights for that matter. It was essentially a dark alley. Planting cameras without being detected would be tricky. She couldn't simply stick a charger in an outdoor wall socket. It would seem pretty out of place. If the nail salon owners were engaged in illegal activity, it was likely that they would find it immediately.

She glanced to her right and studied the eight-foot fence that lined the alley. She turned her vehicle around and exited the parking lot to the left. She needed to find out what was behind that fence.

A smile spread across her face. *Residences.* The fence backed up against people's backyards. Houses meant electrical outlets, but it also meant trespassing on someone's private property. She doubted Martina would approve, but if she could get eyes on the back door, they could learn a lot. Perhaps the neighbors would cooperate and let her plant, cameras, or at least let her go in their backyard? She'd come up with story saying she lost her dog or cat or ... she'd have to think about it more. It was risky. Maybe too risky, but there had to be a way to get eyes on the back door that didn't jeopardize Emily or her own safety.

8

The next night, Selena eased off the gas pedal as she turned down the road just past the strip mall. Outfitted in her most inconspicuous head-to-toe black, including her favorite knit beanie, she was ready to stake out the nail salon. It was only seven o'clock in the evening, but rather dark outside, with only a crescent moon to light the sky.

She couldn't believe how long it took the firm to get the background completed on Pretty Nails owner, Benjie Ocampo, who immigrated to the United States three years ago from the Philippines. Apparently the extra days were necessary to obtain passport photos and a brief background of his life in the Philippines. The photos confirmed the man at the front desk, whom Selena and Dee met, was the owner. Although he had no criminal history in the U.S., his background in the Philippines showed one of a suspected corrupt former policeman.

Selena had gone nearly mad waiting to get back on the case and to stake out the nail salon. Even then, she'd had to beg and plead with Martina to allow it. She'd made her case by explaining that at the nail salon she'd been wearing regular street clothes that were brightly colored with full make-up and her hair flowing. It was a stark contrast to the all-black, no-makeup, and hair-covered look she had now. She could be any young woman.

Martina conceded, but not without requiring her to check in every thirty minutes. Martina had said if she didn't receive a text every thirty minutes, she'd send somebody to check on her. She wondered at what point Martina would allow her to do her job with less checking in. Was it simply because it was her first case or because she was her stepdaughter and worried about her? Or maybe Selena's dad pressured Martina to make sure that Selena stayed safe? Did that mean Martina would always be babysitting her while she was on the job? *I hope not.*

She tucked her car two blocks away from the strip mall, deep in the residential neighborhood. With her baton snug in the pocket of her yoga pants, she was ready for action. She was about to open the door when her cell phone buzzed in her pocket. Who the hell could that be? She slipped it out of her pocket and saw that it was Brendon calling. *Shit.* "Hello."

"Hey. I'm just calling to say hi. I missed you earlier."

Yes, she had to cancel on Brendon to be able to do the stakeout that night. She hadn't told him exactly what she was doing, just that she had to work. She supposed she could have just been honest with him—it would've prevented him from calling her while she was on a stakeout—but after his reaction the previous Saturday night, she started to think the less he knew the better. "I can't really talk right now. Can I call you later?"

"Are you in the office?"

She shut her eyelids and exhaled. "No, I'm out on a stakeout."

There was a prolonged silence from Brendon.

"Brendon?"

He spoke slowly. "Be safe. Selena, I don't know what I would do if I lost you."

"I'm always safe and I can handle myself." Why was everyone so concerned about her? She could take care of herself.

"I know you can. I just can't help but worry. I love you."

She relaxed in the driver's seat. "I love you too. I promise I'll be safe. I'll call you later. I have to go."

"All right, call me soon as you get home, okay?"

"Okay, bye." She hung up without listening to him say good-bye. Great, now she had to check in with Martina *and* Brendon. She'd been through a hell of a lot more than a god damn stakeout, and that was before she'd known self-defense. Now she could take on a guy twice her size. Not only did she have the skills, but she had the element of surprise. They would never see her coming.

She slipped the phone back into her pocket and pulled the handle of her driver's door and stepped out. She strolled down the dark street observing the neighborhood. Middle-class with mid-priced cars in driveways and along the street. Mostly well-kept yards with only a few houses that could use some paint, but in general, a nice, quiet neighborhood. She crossed the road and reached the street where the houses backed up against the strip mall.

When Martina had approved the stakeout, she hadn't approved cameras or Selena sneaking into somebody's backyard to plant them. However, Martina hadn't explicitly stated she couldn't, and Selena didn't say she wouldn't plant cameras. No lies. *Awesome.*

Before trespassing into someone's backyard, she continued down the street to the fence line that bordered the dark alley behind the nail salon and the houses. She peered over and looked down the alley. The back door of Pretty Nails was shut.

At the fence line, she watched for any activity for five

minutes before heading back down toward the street filled with houses. She looked forward to being done planting the cameras and back in her warm car watching the establishment rather than standing there out in the open. She didn't like the exposure and it was freezing outside. Not to mention, she was supposed to be surveilling from her car only. She didn't *like* breaking protocol, but it was necessary in this case.

She made a left down the residential street and hurried toward the third house on the left, the backyard she'd need to access. She studied the front of the house. A fence on the left, presumably with a gate to the backyard. She glanced back over her shoulder and didn't see anyone out on the street. She tiptoed alongside the house, glancing from left to right. She made her way to the gate. She reached her arm over and unhooked the latch.

As soon as she pushed the gate open, she was blinded by a bright light and sounds of a dog barking. *Fuck.* Motion-triggered lighting and a dog. *Shit.* Heart pounding, she eased back and closed the gate as quiet as she could before sprinting back down the street to her car. *Damn it. Damn it. Damn it.*

Now in the safety of her car, she put her hands on the steering wheel and took some cleansing breaths to slow her heart rate. *Cameras were officially too risky.* She started the engine, turned off her headlights, and made a U-turn driving up alongside the fence and parking. *Shit, that was close.*

Her line of sight gave her a visual on the back door of the nail salon. She undid her seatbelt and settled in for what could be a very boring few hours. She texted Martina that she was in position. Martina responded with a thumbs-up emoji.

As she waited and watched basically nothing happening, she tried to put the pieces together. A couple of different scenarios came to mind. Obviously, one scenario was that the parents pretended they took Emily to a nail salon. Maybe Julie

Harrington had been there before and had suspected it was involved in human trafficking, making it a great cover to conceal the fact she and Rick had killed Emily either on purpose or by accident. Not good news for Emily. But if that were the case, why would the Harringtons have hired Drakos Monroe? To see if they could be exposed?

Or a second scenario, the nail salon was a front for a human trafficking ring, which Selena was more and more convinced of each moment, and Emily had been a special order. They grabbed her and sold her to the highest bidder. Unfortunately, if that were the case, Emily may be lost forever.

Or maybe neither of the above? Somebody off the street could've walked into the nail salon and snatched Emily. But then why would the nail salon say she'd never been there?

Or did the Harringtons sell Emily to the traffickers? It wouldn't be the first time parents sold their children into slavery or to the sex trade. But that just didn't quite seem to fit. The Harringtons didn't seem heartless. She could almost see an accidental death, then covering it up with this story about the nail salon, but not actually selling her.

Or somebody could be holding Emily for ransom and just hadn't asked for the money yet. But again, why make up the story about the nail salon if that was the case? Unless the kidnappers had instructed the Harringtons to do so. With virtually zero evidence, none or any of the scenarios could explain the disappearance of seven-year-old Emily. *Frustrating.*

Concern for the girl plagued nearly every thought Selena had. Selena wasn't sure how she'd react if they didn't find her or didn't find her alive. As it was, in the last week she'd only half-paid attention to her classes. Her classes seemed meaningless compared to trying to find Emily.

Selena wondered how her parents would react if she decided to quit school to pursue private investigations full-time. They had never discussed the possibility, but maybe they'd be okay with it? Martina hadn't gone to college, nor had Selena's father, Charlie. However, Martina was ex-military. Between her skills and her connections to the police departments, maybe she hadn't needed extra education.

Was Selena's time better spent actually doing something like finding missing persons or writing essays about crime theory?

Selena picked up her phone and texted another check-in text to Martina. As she was setting her phone back down she saw a flicker of movement from the corner of her eye. Selena stared intently at the figure coming out of the back door of the nail salon. The door was being held open by another person. She could only see the arm, but based on the size and the dark hair, it was likely another man. Ocampo? The figure was tall, middle-aged, in a suit with a loosened tie, walking over to a silver Mercedes parked along the fence directly behind the door to the nail salon. He clicked the fob and opened the car door.

Selena quickly tapped in his license plate number into her phone. Wearing a suit, it was unlikely he was an employee. The vehicle lights turned on and red illuminated the pavement. Probably a john, a guy who justified his time with the poor trafficked woman as being a natural need for men. Or that they were somehow helping them out. *Asshole.* Selena texted Martina the license plate number and a brief description of what she'd witnessed.

Selena continued until eleven o'clock. In that time, she saw nineteen different men, all sizes and races, enter and exit the back door. *There is no fucking way this isn't a secret brothel.* Her blood boiled. The thought of those poor women being defiled by these jerks. She wanted to run out and scream at them, *"What the fuck is wrong with you?"*

She wanted to call the police and have them shut down, but then maybe they'd never find Emily. Not that men coming out of a nail salon in all hours of the night definitively proved it was human trafficking, but between the mattresses, and the man and young woman in the back room, it was pretty clear what was going on. But they still didn't have a connection to Emily.

Before wrapping up for the night, Selena drove to the parking lot and stopped a few rows back from the nail salon, keeping an eye on the parking stalls directly in front of Pretty Nails. By luck or chance, she spotted Ocampo getting into a vehicle. Where was he going? Home? Or did he have additional business to tend to? Or was he just a little fish in a much bigger pond of slimy predators?

She'd already texted Martina that she was going home for the day. It would be too risky to follow him now, wouldn't it? Yes, it would. She needed Martina to trust her, so she couldn't deviate from the approved plan too much. She'd already flubbed placement of the cameras. If she'd been caught, who knows how Martina would've reacted. Not to mention if the homeowner had called the police. It could've blown the entire investigation and they'd never find Emily. It would be her fault. She couldn't allow that.

Selena watched Ocampo drive off in his white Toyota Camry. *I may not get you tonight, jerk face, but one day I will. One day soon.*

9

Selena parked her car in front of the Harringtons' home. Based on the previous evening's surveillance and the background check they'd run on Rick and Julie, it was time to give the couple an update. Not that they'd told the Harringtons the firm was looking into them or tracking their movements. But it was important in order to put all the pieces together. They hadn't found anything out of place in the behavior or financials of the Harringtons. It was likely they weren't involved in Emily's disappearance. Which was good news, considering they were their clients.

Selena shut off the engine and turned to Martina. "Shall we?"

"We shall."

Selena and Martina exited her car and strolled up the walk. Selena gave a quick rap on the door. A few moments passed before the door creaked open. Rick Harrington stood on the other side, not looking any better than the last time they'd met. His shirt was wrinkled and his trousers creased. He wore dark circles under his eyes and his olive skin had a tinge of gray. "Selena, Martina, please come in."

They walked through the entry of the house and stepped into the living room with the two sofas facing one another and a fireplace on the far wall. Julie was sitting on the larger of the two sofas holding the sleeping baby. She didn't look much better either.

As they approached, Rick quietly asked, "Can I get anyone a drink?"

Martina and Selena declined.

Rick said, "Okay. Please have a seat."

Selena sat, hands in her lap. "As I mentioned on the phone, we're here to give you an update on the case."

Before she could finish, Rick interrupted. "Have you received any new information?"

Selena was saddened by his clear desperation to find his daughter. "Not yet. But what we do have is some more information about the nail salon that Emily was taken from."

"You believe me that they took her?" Julie asked with pleading eyes.

"Of course. What we've found is that there appears to be illegal activities going on at the nail salon. We're fairly confident that it is a front for a human trafficking ring. My theory is that the women working there doing the nails have been trafficked from the Philippines, but beyond being forced to work in the nail salon we also believe they are forcing the women into prostitution. We have witnessed men coming in and out of the salon at late hours of the evening. We're fairly certain that is what's going on there."

Rick and Julie turned toward one another as if in shock by the news.

"What does that have to do with … Emily?" Rick Harrington's voice began to crack and then his speech slowed as he seemed to recognize why the traffickers may have wanted to take Emily.

"We still have some things to follow up on in order to make a connection between the people at the nail salon and Emily."

Rick shook his head back and forth. "So we're not really any closer to finding Emily?"

Selena's heart sank. He was clearly disappointed by the news. Before she could protest, Martina spoke. "We have some leads based on what we found that we will investigate further. We actually think this may be a step in the right direction. It'll just take some time."

Rick cried, "We don't have time. Emily doesn't have time."

Selena sensed the parent's nerves were wearing thin. She wasn't sure what their expectations were of how quickly they would find Emily, but they were working as fast as they could. She now regretted not following Ocampo the night before. What if he had Emily stashed somewhere?

Selena looked Rick directly in the eyes. "I promise we will do everything we can to bring Emily home as quickly as possible."

Rick buried his face in his hands, while his wife turned to the side with tears streaming down her cheeks. Their fear and anguish were palpable.

After a few moments, the man raised his head and lowered his hands down to his lap. "I'm sorry. I know you're working as hard as you can. Thank you. It's just been so hard."

A thought popped into Selena's head. "It's okay. But, uh, Mr. Harrington, would you mind if I took a look at Emily's room one more time?" Selena tried to sound as sweet as possible.

Maybe there was something special about Emily that caught the kidnapper's attention and it could help them figure out why she was taken or provide a clue to how to find her.

Rick and Julie exchanged glances.

Selena eyed them both. Why would they be concerned for her to see Emily's room? "Do you mind if we just go upstairs? First room on the left, correct?" Selena asked.

Julie Harrington jumped off the seat, sleeping baby still in her arms. "I'll go with you."

Something was odd about her behavior. Now Selena *really* wanted to see Emily's room.

"Julie, do you want me to take Gemma?" Rick asked.

Julie strengthened her embrace on her child. "No, it's fine." Something was off about Julie's behavior. It was as if she were hiding something.

The four ascended the stairs and reached Emily's room. Julie stepped back and allowed Selena and Martina to enter. Selena looked at the room and refrained from showing any kind of expression of shock or surprise on her face. All of Emily's belongings were now in boxes with the exception of her bed, a dresser with a lamp, an empty bookshelf, and wall hangings. Why would they have boxed up Emily's belongings? The girl had been gone three and a half weeks. Did they not think she was coming back?

Selena eyed Martina.

Martina gave her a knowing look, like *this is not normal*. Martina faced Julie. "Looks like you've done a bit of tidying since we were here last week."

"Yes, I decided to clean up and put the things the police had strewn about into boxes. It was such a mess."

Selena thought it was a strange behavior. Not that she understood what it would be like to have a child go missing, but she would've expected that they would have put Emily's things back the way they were, so that her room would be neat and tidy for her when she returned. That is, if they believed she was coming home. Did they think Emily wasn't coming back?

Selena reexamined her closet and then the bookshelf and dresser. Nothing stood out as to why someone would take her.

"Have you seen everything you need to see?" Julie asked.

Selena said, "Yes, thank you."

Thirty minutes ago, when they had walked up to the front of the house, Selena was sure the Harringtons had nothing to do with their child's disappearance, but now, something didn't feel right. And Selena was going to figure out exactly what it was.

After saying their goodbyes, Martina and Selena drove back to the office. "What do you make of the boxing up of her things? That can't be normal," Selena asked.

"No, I don't think it is. I don't think it means that they're guilty, but it is strange."

"Strange, like they're hoping she doesn't come back?"

"I don't know. I've never been in the situation. I can only imagine what they're going through. But it does seem definitely odd."

Selena wondered if this was the time to suggest cameras at the nail salon and maybe even at the Harringtons' house. She didn't think she'd be able to get away with it on her own. She spoke as casually as possible. "Do you think it would be a good idea to get cameras on the nail salon or even the Harrington home?" Selena watched Martina from the corner of her eye.

Martina's lips parted as if she was about to speak but then stopped herself. A few moments passed before Martina spoke. "This is a different ballgame out here, Selena. Planting cameras at a fraternity is one thing, but these are traffickers. You mess that up and you may find yourself disappearing without a trace. Promise me right now, you will not try to go on your own and attempt to plant cameras." Martina gave Selena a stern look.

Selena swallowed. "I won't. But do you have guys that maybe could?"

"It's too risky at this point. There aren't a lot of places to hide them and the nail salon is likely on high alert since the police searched them after Emily was taken and now that they've seen you in the back room."

Selena thanked her lucky stars that she hadn't gotten caught with those cameras the night before. She'd seen Martina serious before, but the look she now gave her ... Selena would definitely not be planting cameras *any time* soon.

The air was thick with tension. They didn't speak for several minutes. It was almost as if Martina knew that's exactly what she'd tried to do.

"Is Dee fully trained now?" Martina asked.

Selena let out the breath she didn't know she was holding. "I showed her the basics yesterday before I went on the stakeout. She's a pretty quick study." Dee was smart and it wasn't a difficult job. The most difficult thing about it was not falling asleep while you were doing it.

"Excellent. Maybe for tonight's stakeout you can take her along. I'd feel better if there were two of you instead of one. But make sure she's in disguise, obviously. I probably don't need to tell you that."

No, you don't need to tell me that. "I'll talk to her and ask her."

"Great."

The case against the traffickers was strong, but the connection to Emily was not. Selena needed to change that, and fast.

10

Selena assumed her position along the fence line behind the back of the nail salon. She sat in the driver's seat while Dee rode shotgun. Tonight was no different than the previous night. A steady stream of johns exiting the back door, leaving in their fancy cars. At least this time she had Dee to keep her company, record the license plates, and take pictures. She liked having an assistant. She liked being in charge. And she liked the company. Dee asked, "Is this what it's like to be a private investigator? You sit in the car and watch people all night?"

"It's a little bit more than that, but there is a lot of waiting. Put it this way, I now understand why, when I first started, Martina explained that patience was a critical attribute to being a private investigator. And usually there's not anybody here with me, so thanks for coming along."

"No problem. Kind of interesting but also heartbreaking that so many people in the community are coming to this nail salon and violating these women."

"Yeah, it's pretty disgusting. It's almost as if these men have no respect for their fellow humans."

Dee nodded. "Yeah, lots of men out there not respecting women."

Selena paused before asking Dee the next question on her mind. She'd been wanting to broach the subject, but wasn't sure if Dee was ready to discuss it. It been more than a year since Dee's attack and she hadn't dated or even mentioned a man's name in reference to a romantic interest. "Are you, uh, still not interested in dating?"

Dee shook her head. "No, not at all. I'm just not ready to date. Maybe I'll never be ready."

It was sad, but she understood. Everybody healed at their own pace. "Do you miss dating at all?"

"Not really. I didn't date a lot when I was in high school and to be honest, I keep pretty busy, so I don't ever feel like, 'hey I wish I was going out with some guy.' Between school, volunteering at the center, and now working with you, my time is pretty full."

"You like working at the center?"

Dee shrugged. "Yes. I wish I could do more. Lately, I've been thinking maybe I'll end up becoming a psychiatrist and help victims on a mental level versus the physical level."

"Wow. That would be awesome. A lot of work though, right?"

Dee laughed lightly. "It is a lot of work. I mean between lecture and labs, I feel like I'm doing twice as much work as non-science majors. But that's the road I've taken. It's not too bad. It'll be worth it in the end."

"That's great. I think that anything you decide to do that you love, can't be wrong."

"Yeah, I feel pretty good about it. Speaking of boys ... How are things with you and Brendon? He seems like such a good boyfriend."

He was. She wondered how good of a girlfriend she'd been

lately. "Yeah, he's funny though. He really wants to celebrate Valentine's Day. I mean, it's silly, right? It's a made-up holiday."

"No, it's sweet and he's a romantic. You know that about him. He's very sensitive. And he is head over heels in love with you. Hey, if he wants to take you out for a Valentine's Day dinner and give you a box of chocolate, why would you fight it? If you don't want the candy, I'll take it off your hands for you." Dee winked at her.

"I suppose you have a point." And she really loved Brendon. She felt guilty that she canceled their last two dates because she was working on the case. He seemed to understand, but people were only understanding up to a point.

Dee pointed to a vehicle pulling into the lot. "We've got another one."

Selena's mouth dropped open and her pulse raced when the car stopped.

Dee said, "Hey, it's a woman. That's a first, right?"

Holy shit. It wasn't just any woman. "That's Julie Harrington."

"Emily's mother?"

Selena clarified with a suspicious tone. "Emily's *stepmother*." What the hell was Julie doing at the nail salon? Selena ducked back as Dee took photos. Julie didn't leave her vehicle, and from the looks of it, she was alone in the car.

Ocampo exited the back door a minute later and approached the driver's side door. Words were exchanged before Ocampo headed back to the nail salon and Julie quickly drove off. What the hell was going on? Had Julie been paid to let them take Emily? Were they somehow in business together? Was Julie Harrington part of the trafficking ring?

11

Selena widened her eyes to force them open. It was after midnight and she'd had far too much caffeine that appeared to stop taking effect hours ago. She shook her head to stir her mind awake. She wasn't going to miss the opportunity to follow Ocampo, presumably the leader of the trafficking operation, after he left the nail salon for the night.

After Dee and Selena had witnessed Julie Harrington meeting with Ocampo at Pretty Nails, she'd wanted to run over to the Harrington home and demand to know what was going on. Martina had talked her down from that ledge by promising to put a tail back on the Harringtons and explaining that confronting Julie didn't mean that they would find Emily and could even put her in further danger.

If Julie had sold Emily or had willingly given her away, going after her may alert the traffickers and they may never rescue Emily, assuming she was still alive. Selena tried to bury the anger and rage toward the woman. The fact that Julie had been alone made Selena believe that Rick was not involved, but who knew, maybe they were both total creeps. Maybe they were gonna raise the new child and sell that one as well? Maybe it was their very own sick and twisted business venture.

"You okay over there?" Dee asked.

Selena stared out the window at the front of the salon. "Yeah, I'll make it. They'll be closing up shop soon. Once they do, it's go time." She turned to face Dee. "You sure you're okay with this? It could get dangerous if they catch us."

Dee tugged at her black baseball cap. "I'll be fine. I have my pepper spray and my self-defense training. And since we aren't leaving the car, it's pretty low-risk, right?"

Selena was grateful that Dee had taken her advice and learned basic self-defense. Selena thought it was something every woman should know, because you never know when you'll come face-to-face with one of the monsters, especially since they tended to look like everyone else.

Selena eyed the front door of the nail salon, and then slapped Dee on the arm. "There he is. Right there." Selena waited for the man to get into his four-door sedan and hopefully lead them to where he was keeping Emily, assuming she was still with them. It was what one may call a leap of faith. She hoped to god Emily was still with him in the Bay Area, because if she wasn't, the likelihood they'd ever find her diminished severely.

Martina had warned Selena to not form conclusions without all the evidence, but Selena's gut was telling her Ocampo would lead her to Emily. She still wasn't quite sure how the Harringtons were involved. She'd pretty much convinced herself that they weren't—right up until the moment she saw Julie Harrington meeting with Ocampo the previous night.

As Ocampo backed out of the parking stall and drove out of the strip mall parking lot, Selena flicked on her headlights and followed roughly three car lengths behind. Both she and Dee were silent as they followed. She'd never been in pursuit of a suspect before. She felt as if she'd sucked down a sugary Frappuccino with an extra ten shots of espresso. She was amped.

The goal of the mission was to get an address and take a few photos, if he led them somewhere other than his home. One of the other teams had been staking out his house in San Bruno since the day they'd retrieved his address. Based on the surveillance reports, Benjie Ocampo, husband and father of two, didn't mix business with his home life. From the outside, he was just like every other guy living the American dream. But when Selena and the house surveillance team compared notes, they realized Ocampo wasn't going straight home after locking up the nail salon. Therefore, anywhere other than his residence may be the location where he conducted his undercover business. His after-hours location could crack the case wide open.

Martina had been strict about the goals of the surveillance operation that night, claiming that anything other than capturing photos from the safety of their vehicle was far too dangerous. Selena had insisted that she knew how to take care of herself and since Dee was trained, they'd be fine.

They managed to keep close to Ocampo for the next fifteen minutes as they drove on the freeway heading south toward the city of Burlingame. Ocampo took the first exit into Burlingame without using his blinker. Selena had to merge across two lanes to not lose him and to exit the highway.

On the two-lane city streets, it became clear to Selena that it was one thing to follow someone on a large highway, but it was quite another on side streets. With limited street lighting and narrow roads, at nearly one in the morning, not being spotted would be trickier than she'd expected.

Despite the lack of cover, Ocampo didn't seem to notice or be bothered by their vehicle following. Either the guy was cocky and didn't think anybody was onto him or he simply wasn't paying attention.

Selena slowed as he turned right onto a residential street lined with mature trees and older homes, barely wide enough for a car to pass in both directions. She eased off the gas and let him reach his destination. There were no streetlights, and Selena's headlights shined brightly. She flicked off the lights and watched as he reduced his speed and turned into a driveway in front of a house four doors down. She stopped the car and parked. She turned to Dee. "I'm going to get the address on foot. It's too risky with the headlights."

Dee raised her brows. "I thought we were supposed to stay in the car?"

"You stay in the car. I'll be right back." She knew it was off plan and Martina wouldn't be pleased, but there was no way they could get the house number without being spotted with headlights. They would stick out like a sore thumb.

She slowly opened her door and held it so it would close softly, letting it rest in the door frame. She waved silently to Dee before crouching down. She hunched as she ran along the road until the house number was in her sights. *48615.* She stepped back behind a bush and entered the digits into the notes app on her phone. She slid the phone back into her pocket and eased forward and listened.

Three soft knocks on a solid door. Within moments, the door creaked open. Foreign words were exchanged before Ocampo entered, quickly closing the door behind him.

Whose house was it? She supposed they'd find out when they ran the property records. But what were they doing at one in the morning?

Selena was about to turn around and head back to the car when she realized the opportunity that was in front of her. What if they were holding Emily inside? The property records would *not* reveal that critical information.

It was dark out and she was in head-to-toe black. She should be able to sneak around and take a peek inside the house without being seen. Assuming there were no motion sensors or dogs out in the yard. Like last time.

She hunched and scurried along the driveway to the side of the house. Steps descended to the front door, and it was now clear the house was built on the side of a hill. This would make it trickier to get eyes inside the house. But not impossible. *Bingo*. There was no fence, but there was no telling how large the house actually was. The front of the house looked like a modest ranch-style home with wood siding and a two-car garage, but depending on how many levels it was, the home could be fifteen hundred square feet or five thousand square feet.

She stepped down through bushes to a path that ran along the side of the house. She walked quietly, crouching alongside the house. Luckily, she was wearing boots with grippy soles. She slowly peered into the first window on the side of the house, an unused sitting room. It was dark. She continued down the side of the house until she reached a lit window. So far, so good. No motion lights. No pets.

She stood on her tiptoes to take a peek. Inside was a large tan L-shaped sofa with a round coffee table in front of it. On the end of the couch, a middle-aged Caucasian man with a gray goatee and black polo shirt sat holding a tumbler filled with amber-colored liquid. His blue eyes widened and he stood up rather quickly. He placed his glass on the coffee table and stared ahead. His face brightened as a smile crept up his face.

Selena followed his focus. Her body froze and her heart pounded. In the corner stood two figures, Ocampo and another Asian man. The other man leaned against the wall as a young girl approached. She couldn't have been more than five years old. She had mousy brown hair and was wearing a headband adorned with a large pink bow. Her eyes were sleepy, as if she'd been drugged. She was dressed in a frilly pink dress like one you'd see on an old-fashioned doll. She slowly twirled around with a blank look on her face.

Selena returned her gaze to the man with the goatee. He looked like it was Christmas morning and he'd received just the gift he'd asked for. It took everything inside of Selena to not break through the window and beat the man senseless. Who was this little girl?

The man approached and spoke to the girl. The girl nodded. This went on for a few minutes, before the girl was ushered out of the room by the man Selena assumed was Ocampo's partner.

Ocampo approached the man with the gray goatee. Both men smiled as they shook hands. They'd just made a business deal.

Selena held her stomach, willing herself not to be sick. *Vile creatures.* She needed to leave. She needed to call this in. She turned to go back to the car, but was stunned when two large hands grabbed her shoulders. Instinctively she kicked her leg back into the person's crotch and came around, swinging an uppercut to the attacker's chin. Dazed, she pulled out her baton while he was bent over. Before she could get a good swing, he launched his massive fist at her and clocked her on the side of the face. She fell against the side of the house. She steadied herself on the house with one hand and swung her baton wildly with the other. After a few solid sounds indicating the baton made contact, she peeked over her shoulder. The man was bent over.

Her body shook as adrenaline soared.

She whacked the baton on the back of his head, neck, and back until he crumpled, face-down onto the ground. She stared at the defeated monster. There was more blood than she'd expected. She shook her head. *No time to think about that.*

She sprinted back to the car. When she reached it, she flung the door open and jumped into the driver seat. She turned on the engine, drove into the nearest driveway, and backed out before she sped down the street.

"Oh my god! You're bleeding. What happened?" Dee asked.

Selena raised her fingers to the side of her face. It was wet. She stared at her fingers. "We need to get out of here."

"Are you okay?"

"I'll be okay." The man who attacked her, she wasn't so sure about.

12

———

Out of breath, Selena sped onto the highway. From the corner of her eye she saw a white tissue. She accepted it and said, "Thanks." She held it to the side of her face with one hand as she continued to steer with the other. As her head pounded, she could only think of what would happen to that girl. Who was she? Was there a team looking for her? Where was Emily?

"What happened, Selena?" Dee asked with desperation in her voice.

She said, "Very bad things ..." and then went on to explain what she'd witnessed at the house with the men, the girl, and the details of her attack.

Dee was silent.

Selena removed the tissue from her temple. She crumbled the bloody tissue and stuffed it in the middle console. She turned to Dee, whose fair skin now looked nearly translucent. "Should I call the police? I mean, I don't want to incriminate myself, but I can't just let that girl be sold to that man! We can't just let it happen, and time is of the essence. What if they heard the fight and are moving her? I knocked out the guy cold, but that doesn't mean they won't be looking for him. We may only have a few minutes before they could be gone forever."

Dee shook her head. "What if what you saw isn't what you think it is? I mean, what if it's the man's daughter or his granddaughter and just happens to be friends with those guys?"

Selena glanced over at Dee. "You don't really think that, do you?"

"No, but I mean, sometimes things aren't as they seem. Maybe you should call Martina."

Selena should call Martina and explain. Would it risk her career with Drakos Monroe? Not to mention how upset her stepmother and dad would be when they found out what she'd done. But this was a child. The girl's life was more important than her stepmother being mad at her. "Good idea. Can you call her on your cell and I'll talk to her on speaker. I'm already a ball of nerves, I can't be driving while on the phone too."

The light from Dee's phone lit up the car's interior as she called Martina.

Selena focused her eyes on the road. She could hear the sound of ringing from the passenger side. Dee said, "Hi, Martina. No, we're fine. I swear." Another pause. "No, but there's something that happened that Selena needs to tell you. I'll hold up the phone and put you on speaker. She's driving. She'll explain."

Selena leaned into the phone, now inches from her mouth. "Hi Martina, first of all, don't be mad, but I followed Ocampo to a house in Burlingame. I went on foot to get a better look at the house. We have an address, but I looked into the windows and I saw a girl, about five years old, being paraded as if on display, as if for sale. The man shook hands with Ocampo after the girl was taken away. What do I do? Call the police?"

"Can you describe the girl in more detail? I'm gonna pull up the missing child database."

That's it? No lecture? No, Martina must understand the urgency. For sure, the lecture would come later.

Selena described the girl in detail.

She could hear Martina tapping the keys on her computer keyboard over the phone. The car was silent as they waited for Martina to return from her research.

Selena's heart rate began to slow, closer to normal. Her head throbbed. *Shit.* Did she have a concussion? Maybe she shouldn't be driving.

Martina spoke quickly. "I'm texting over a couple of pictures. Pull the car over and take a look. Tell me if any of them are the girl you saw."

"Okay, I'll pull over at the next exit. It's right ahead and I see a gas station." She exited the highway and stopped the car in front of the gas station. She put the car into park. Dee handed her the phone and she studied the first picture. *No.* The next picture. Another cherubic-looking young girl. *No.* The third. "Oh my god. Number three. That's her. I mean she looks a hell of a lot happier in this picture, but that's her. I'd swear by it. It's her." Her heart raced. The pain was once again forgotten and now her only focus was to help this little girl.

Martina said, "That's five-year-old Penny David. She was abducted two months ago from her home in Palo Alto."

"We should call the police, right, Martina? I mean, I don't want to jeopardize finding Emily, but that little girl ... I just can't not do something."

"Of course. Call 9-1-1. Try doing it anonymously."

Selena nodded. "Will do."

"Give me a call when you get home, so I know you've made it there safely, okay?"

"You got it."

She hung up the phone and dialed 9-1-1. She explained to the operator that she'd had a sighting of the missing five-year-old, Penny David and gave them the address where she'd been last seen. Selena prayed to god they weren't too late.

Hope filled Selena. If they took Penny two months ago and they hadn't killed her, Emily could still be alive.

13

———

Selena entered Drakos Monroe the next morning with an uneasy feeling in her gut. She faked a smile to Mrs. Pearson, the receptionist, and continued on back to the conference room where Martina was waiting for her. The entire week she'd been working on the Emily Harrington case, Martina had not demanded she come down to the office for a formal meeting. And this one was without explanation. She entered conference room two, the largest of the conference rooms in the office. A large oval table sat in the center with twelve executive-style chairs surrounding the table. The walls were adorned with whiteboards and dry-erase markers.

Martina sat on the other side of the table staring at her laptop screen and typing on the keyboard. She took off her reading glasses and placed them on the table before standing up. "Hi Selena, thank you for coming down here today. I know it wasn't planned, but I thought it would best if we met in person."

So formal. Never a good sign. "No problem."

Martina tipped her chin. "Do you need coffee or water or anything else before we get started?"

"No, I'm fine." Selena took a seat next to Martina and put her shoulder bag onto the ground. She slipped out her laptop and set it on the table. Martina shut the door and returned to her seat. Why did she feel like she had been sent to the principal's office? Not that she had ever really gotten in trouble at school, but she had a feeling this was what it would've felt like if she had.

Martina gave her a reassuring smile. "How's your head? It looks swollen. Have you gone to the hospital?"

Selena shook her head. "No, it's fine. I put some ice on it earlier."

Martina turned serious. "Have you had any dizziness? Nausea? Headache? Vomiting? Confusion?"

"No, I mean, it's sore, but I feel fine." Other than feeling stupid for being caught off guard by the man, but that wasn't a physical pain. So really, she was fine.

Martina scrunched up her face as if she weren't convinced. "You're sure?"

"I'm fine."

"Okay, well, you showed good investigative instincts last night—and you saved a girl's life. Have you heard the news that Penny David was reunited with her family a few hours ago? I talked to a buddy of mine at Burlingame PD and they arrested the man with the goatee, Lester Devenworth. He was the owner of the house, but by the time the police arrived, Ocampo and partner were in the wind."

Selena had to stop her jaw from dropping to the floor. This wasn't a lashing? "Yeah, it's great news. It's just too bad they didn't find Emily or Ocampo."

Martina turned serious. "No mistake, you did great work, but it was also incredibly dangerous. You broke protocol. You could've been killed. And as much as I want to find Emily, your life is more important to me."

Selena touched the side of her forehead, which was throbbing once again. "But I wasn't."

Martina remained stoic. "How many hours have you spent on the case this week, Selena?"

Selena glanced up to calculate the time. She spent all her evenings, but hadn't missed any of her classes. She did homework during the day on the weekends. All other time was devoted to the case. "I don't know, maybe six or seven hours each night for the stakeouts, meeting with the family, reviewing surveillance reports ... Maybe forty or fifty hours total last week."

Martina frowned. "Selena, that's too much. We made an agreement when you took this job. School is your number-one priority, not working. I have to admit, when I gave you this case, I thought it would be much smaller in scope. As awful as it sounds, I assumed the girl was dead. I thought you'd be able to put together some clues as to maybe where her body was buried and you could bring closure to the family." She paused and shook her head. "What you've discovered is that it's a much, much larger case. Between human trafficking, the brothel, the kidnapping and selling of young girls, and now potentially with the parents being involved? This is a huge case, Selena. I want to bring Emily Harrington, assuming she's still alive, either home or at least make sure that she's safe. Usually, loyalty goes to our clients, but if they're guilty in the disappearance, or are somehow associated with the disappearance of Emily, we do what's right here at Drakos Monroe. And what's right is making sure Emily is found. I know this was supposed to be your first case, but I'm afraid I need to step in and play a more active role."

A more active role? Heat seared through her. "That's not fair. I can do this. I can keep up with school and find Emily."

Martina shook her head. "School needs to be your top priority, and we have a priority at this firm to find Emily. Look, here's what I'm willing to do. I have a team in charge of surveilling

Julie and Rick Harrington, Ocampo, and the nail salon. This is a full-time job for all the people I have assigned to the case."

Selena shook her head in disbelief. Writing another essay on the history of the justice system was more important than finding Emily? *No fucking way.*

Martina locked onto her. "Let me finish. I'm willing to let you help run point. You'll have access to all the intelligence gathered, attend briefings, and discuss theories. Essentially, you'll be the brains of the operations. But no more stakeouts. No more surveillance."

Selena folded her arms across her chest and pursed her lips. "This doesn't make sense, Martina. I can do the job full-time. I've been doing it. And the more I think about it, do I really need a degree? You don't have one, and neither does Dad."

She stared at Martina as her chest heaved.

Martina's face had grown pale and serious. "Selena, what are your career aspirations? Do you want to be a private investigator who investigates cases for the rest of your life? If the answer is yes, you're right. If all you want to do is be a private investigator, you don't need to finish school. You have great instincts. I'll think you'll be great. But don't you want more?"

"Yes. I do want more than just investigating cases. I want to be running investigations, directing people, and leading teams. If I go into private investigations instead of law enforcement, I want to be a partner, like you."

Martina sat back and her expression softened. "If that's the case, here's what I'll say. Although that is true, I don't have a college degree, I do have military training, which taught me leadership and how to command a team. I'm not suggesting you go into the military, but if you really would like to have a leader-ship role in this firm one day—after of course you've mastered both private investigations as well as the security side—you could become a partner in this firm. But know this, being a partner is more than just experience in the field. This is where your education can play a role. You need leadership and business experience. My recommendation is you either remain a criminal justice major and minor in business, or since you're only in your second year, you can change your major and still probably graduate on time, change your major to business management with a criminal justice minor. Either way, I recommend you take some business classes. Leadership. Finance. Accounting. Economics. All the subjects you'll need to know to run a business. I don't just lead teams, Selena, I also run the business. There's a whole lot of stuff that goes on behind the scenes that mean a degree would be incredibly beneficial for you and also would make you stand out against other candidates in a leadership role."

Selena was about to protest once again and give her two cents, when Martina raised her hand to stop her. "And one more thing. On a personal level, your mother didn't have a college degree. Your father doesn't have a college degree. College isn't just about the subjects that you learn, it's also about gaining perspective in order to see the world in a different view. Your father is so proud of you, as am I. You should be proud of yourself for going to college. If you stay, you'll be the first person in your family to earn a degree. That is not something to take lightly. Education is something nobody can ever take away from you. Remember that. *Education is a gift.*"

Selena sunk back into her chair and thought over what Martina was saying to her. She wanted to be an investigator. She also wanted to be a leader and a businessperson like Martina. She *also* wanted to find Emily Harrington.

"I can still be a part of the case?"

Martina cocked her head. "Yes, but no more going rogue. This case has become far too dangerous and I'm not willing to let my stepdaughter get killed."

She wasn't completely pulled from her case, but it still sucked. She was only allowed to investigate from the office. An armchair detective. She'd been benched. She'd need some of that private investigator patience to kick in. *Soon.* "Okay. No more going rogue."

"You know you have a full-time job here as soon as you graduate, right?"

Selena nodded.

"I'll expect you in the office to have regular meetings with the team, to talk strategy, and review evidence."

"What about interviewing Julie? She met with Ocampo! She has to be involved somehow."

"I think we need to tread lightly with Julie Harrington. We'll keep our eyes on her. Whatever she's up to, we might be able to catch her in the act."

Selena sat quietly staring at the floor.

"Are you okay?"

"I'm just disappointed. I like being in the field and I really want to find Emily, but I'll consider what you said about school."

"We will find Emily. We have great leads thanks to you. And you know that if you have any questions about this job, I'm more than happy to answer them. Be warned, there's a lot of boring stuff that I do as a partner in the firm. Last preaching of the day, I promise. I strongly believe that you should stay in school. Get your degree. Graduate."

Selena nodded in acknowledgement.

Martina said, "Are you ready to talk strategy?"

Finally. "Yes, let's do it."

After an hour-long strategy session, Selena left the office with a little more pep in her step and the first night off in a week. And she knew just the six-foot cutie she'd like to hang out with. Getting benched didn't have to be all bad.

14

Selena fidgeted outside of Brendon's apartment as she waited for him to let her in. The door swung open and an involuntary grin crept up her face. She stepped in and wrapped her arms around his neck, kissing him a little more passionately than she had planned. She unlocked her lips and stared into his eyes. "I missed you so much."

"I missed you too." He gave her another quick peck before untangling himself from her to shut the front door. He refocused on her and his face fell. "What happened to your face?"

She traced the now bandaged bump with her fingers. "Oh that. A bit of a scuffle."

His eyes widened. "A scuffle?"

"It's a long story. I'm fine, really."

He didn't seem convinced as she continued into the hall of his small apartment. She glanced to her left and saw Glenn, Brendon's roommate on the couch. She waved. Glenn gave her a head nod before returning his focus to his video game.

Brendon took Selena's hand and led her back to his bedroom, where he sat her down on the bed. He sat next to her. "Now, tell me about this scuffle."

Selena inhaled and exhaled. "Okay, so ..." She told him everything from seeing Penny David at the house in Burlingame to the attack by the unknown man outside that same house.

Brendon's eyes grew wide. "You could've been killed."

"I wasn't killed. I'm fine. Barely a scratch." It didn't erase the worry from his face. It seemed to only make it worse. "I know how to defend myself. I was just shocked by what I saw and I let my guard down for a second."

Brendon shook his head back and forth. "That's all it takes is a second. What if he had a gun?"

Then she would be dead. Her job was a dangerous one, but she couldn't just stand by and not help these women and young girls. She knew the danger they were in. She couldn't simply look the other way and pretend it wasn't happening.

Brendon stood up from the bed and began pacing around the room. She waited for him to say something—something good. The long face, the sad eyes. It was more than she could take. She found herself pleading with him. "I'll be careful next time, I promise."

He stopped pacing. "Next time? You're not even twenty years old. What you're doing is real and dangerous. I'm worried about you and this line of work. I know you can take care of yourself, but the idea of losing you. I just ..." He stared down at the ground.

Selena tried to put herself in Brendon's shoes. Would she be okay with dating someone with a dangerous job? Yes. Would she worry? Yes. But if it was his passion, she would have to support it, right? A lot of people had dangerous jobs and maintained relationships. Why should she be any different? Was he being overly sensitive because she was a female?

She would've loved to blame the patriarchy for this one, but the despair emanating from Brendon nearly broke her heart. He was genuinely concerned about her. She supposed it wasn't unreasonable. If her attacker had a gun, he could've shot her dead. There was no denying that. She'd have to be more careful next time. *Always be on guard.* It was like Martina always told her, experience trumped everything out in the field. No amount of training in a gymnasium could make up for real-world experience. *Wasn't that the truth.*

She walked over to him and wrapped her arms around his neck. "I'll be okay. I promise. Nothing is going to happen to me. Plus, Martina pulled me from field work. Just a desk job for this gal, for now."

He met her gaze. "Really?"

Was he too happy about that? "Really."

He placed his hands on her hips. "Does that mean we can celebrate Valentine's Day together? No cancellations?"

"When is Valentine's Day?"

"Next Friday."

She begged the Universe that they'd find Emily by Friday. She nodded and smiled. "I promise."

"And no work tonight?"

"Nope. I'm all yours."

He gave her a devilish grin. "Really?"

She beamed up at him and said, "Really," before she unwrapped her arms from around his neck, took him by the hand and led him back over to the bed.

The next morning, Selena kissed Brendon and then waved goodbye as she stepped over the threshold of the front door out on to the porch. She descended the steps and headed over to the side street where she'd parked. She approached the car and froze. She knelt down on one knee and inspected the back tire. *Flat.* She crept forward toward the passenger side front tire. *Flat.*

She quickly scurried over to driver's side of the car. All four tires were flat. Had someone slashed her tires? Was this the handiwork of some bored kids? Or had the traffickers sent her a message?

She rushed toward the car parked in front of hers to see if their tires were flat. *Nope.* She continued to the next and the next, before turning back. *Only my tires are flat.* Her pulse quickened.

Selena hurried back up to Brendon's apartment and explained to him she had a flat tire and *not* her theory it may be the trafficker's sending her a message.

"Do you have a spare?"

A spare? Yes. Four spares? No. "No, I'm just going to call the auto club and have them tow it to a tire shop and have them replaced."

Brendon cocked his head. "Them replaced? How many flat tires do you have?"

Shit. She couldn't lie to him. "It's all four."

All the color drained from his face. "Selena. What if this is related to the case? They know who you are and where I live— probably where you live too!"

"Or it was some bored kids." She tried her best to sound convincing, but she was sure she'd failed. Hard.

Brendon shook his head, clearly not believing her less awful scenario. Mostly because she wasn't buying it either. He was absolutely correct. The criminals she was investigating now likely knew the car she drove and where Brendon lived. Did they know her identity too? *Shit.* What if her visiting Brendon put him in danger? It would be her fault if something happened to him. She'd been too careless. She had to fix this.

She wrapped her arms around Brendon and embraced him in a tight hug. Then she whispered in his ear. "I'll get this straightened out, okay? I'm sure we're overreacting."

He brushed a stray hair from her face and tucked it behind her ear. "I hope you're right, but I don't think so. Please, I need you to be careful. I can't lose you."

"I don't want to lose you either."

As they waited for the tow truck, Selena and Brendon sat on the edge of his bed holding hands, not wanting to be more than an inch away from one another. The only thing Selena could think was, *fingers crossed it was just bored kids.*

15

Selena trudged into her house and dropped her tote bag onto the floor in the hall before heading to the sofa and plopping down with a heavy sigh. What a day. After three hours at the tire shop, she finally had a vehicle capable of driving on the road. Ugh. Not something she'd like to have to do again.

Dee strolled into the living room, said, "Hey. How's it going?" And then curled up on the sofa next to her.

Selena took a deep breath. "It's been better," she said and went on to explain to Dee everything that had happened that morning.

Dee's mouth dropped open. "What does Martina have to say about all of this?"

"I haven't told her."

"What? You could be in danger. I could be in danger. This whole house could be in danger. Brendon too. And what about the rest of the team at Drakos Monroe? If they know who you are, then they know where you work. The whole team could be at risk."

Selena hadn't considered that. "I don't know. You think? Nobody else has had any kind of message or attack."

"As far as you know."

She thought Dee may be overreacting. She didn't even know if the flat tires were a message, but Dee had a point about calling Martina. She should know, on the off chance it was the traffickers sending a message to Selena and the rest of the Drakos Monroe team. Before she could pick up her phone to call Martina, her cell phone buzzed. She stared down at it on the sofa cushion next to her. *Unknown caller.* Something told her to pick it up. "Hello."

"Did you get our message from this morning?"

Selena froze. *Shit.* Heart pounding, she said, "Yes."

"Just so we're very clear, Selena Bailey, not only do we know who you are, but we also know all about your boyfriend, Brendon Vale. You let this go, or it's goodbye Mr. Vale. Do you understand, Selena?"

"Yes, I understand." Her body rattled as adrenaline soared through her body. She'd been told no more fieldwork, but they just threatened her boyfriend and that was *not* okay. She was going down to the nail salon and she was going down there *today.*

Dee stood there staring at Selena with her hands on her hips. "Who the hell was that?"

"It was them. The traffickers. I'm going to go talk to them. Nobody threatens the people I care about."

"What do you mean? Where are you going?"

"I'm going down to the nail salon to talk to Ocampo."

Dee shook her head. "It's too dangerous, Selena!"

"They know my name. They probably know where I live. They know where Brendon lives. The danger already exists. It's time I talk to them face-to-face and end this."

"Selena, I think this is a really bad idea. I think you should call Martina at a minimum and get some backup."

"It's the middle of the day. It'll be fine. I just want to talk to

Ocampo and let him know I'm not backing down. They need to know I'm serious."

"I don't think you understand that this is organized crime. They're not afraid of you or any other single person. I'm your best friend and you know I wouldn't lie to you. I'm telling you right now, this is foolish. Call Martina."

Selena shook her head. "I can handle it." She wasn't exactly sure what she would say or do when she faced off with Ocampo, but what she did know was that she couldn't let anything happen to Brendon. It would destroy her.

She stood up and glanced down at Dee. "I'll call you later." Selena grabbed her keys from the end table and her jacket from the hook in the hall and stormed out of their house. These assholes were not getting away with this. Not on her watch.

16

Selena parked in the stall directly in front of Pretty Nails. Taser in her back pocket and baton in her front, she powered toward the glass doors of the nail salon. She flung one open and stormed to the counter. She stood face-to-face with Benjie Ocampo, who was standing behind the reception desk. He gave her the same crooked smile as the first time she'd been there. She spat, "I have a message for you."

He gave her a confused look. "I'm sorry. Do you have an appointment?"

Selena inched closer. "I said, I have a message for you."

"Maybe you have the wrong place. I don't know you. I don't know what message you're referring to."

Selena leaned forward and pointed her finger. "I know you took Emily. I know that these women here are being trafficked. If you don't back away and leave me and everyone I care about alone, you will be sorry." Her body shook with rage. She was so angry, she had to use every bit of self-restraint to not pull out her baton and bash in the man's face.

Ocampo stepped back and feigned innocence. "I'm sorry,

Miss, I don't know what you're talking about. Did you want to get a manicure or a pedicure?"

He was toying with her. He knew exactly what she was talking about. And she had a pretty damn good idea that he knew exactly who she was. Hands on hips, she warned, "Stay away from my family *and* my friends."

He walked around the desk and opened the front door and held it open for her. The cold air sent shivers down her spine.

Ocampo said, "Miss, I'm afraid if you aren't here for a manicure or a pedicure, I'm going to have to ask you to leave."

Selena stood within inches of his body. With chest heaving, she vowed, "I will get Emily back."

Ocampo squinted down at her and spoke in a low, hushed tone. "*Selena*, if you're so concerned about Emily, why don't you go talk to her daddy?"

Selena stepped back.

Ocampo leaned toward her, inches from her face. Selena could feel his hot breath against her face. He whispered, " Don't come back here, or you will be the one who is sorry. That I promise."

Selena exited and hurried over to her car. Was she in over her head? And what the hell had Ocampo meant about talking to Emily's daddy? Was Rick Harrington somehow involved? *Only one way to find out.*

17

Selena pounded on the door with her fist three times before it flung open. Rick Harrington appeared, looking shaken. "Selena, what are you doing here?"

"I'm here for answers." She stormed in without being invited. She paced his living room. "What the hell is going on, Mr. Harrington? I was just at the nail salon. And guess what? They said I should talk to you. How are you involved? Where's Julie?"

Rick shook his head vigorously. "You need to leave."

"I'm not going anywhere until you tell me what's going on. Whatever you and Julie have done is now affecting my loved ones. They've threatened me and my boyfriend. I find this utterly unacceptable. If you are involved, you'd better tell me *now*." She now had her baton in her hand ready to retract. She was getting answers one way or another.

He stepped closer, and under his breath he said, "You're going to get her killed. Please. Leave."

Her body went rigid. In that moment she knew a few things. One, Emily was still alive and two, somehow Rick had been in touch with the traffickers. Three, he had not sold Emily. Why hadn't he told them he'd been contacted by the kidnappers? She met his gaze. "We can help you."

"You're fired. Please leave."

Selena shook her head. "I'm not leaving until you tell me what is going on. You hired us to find your daughter and we will, with or without you."

"You need to leave now, or I will remove you."

He was pale and his body shook. He seemed scared, but not of her. What the hell was going on?

She stormed out of the house and he shut the door quickly behind her. She headed to her car and slipped into the driver seat. Had they received a ransom demand? Had Julie sold Emily and now Rick was trying to get her back? Before she could turn the key into the ignition. Her cell phone buzzed. *Crap*. It was Martina. "Hello?"

Martina said, "What the hell are you doing? My guys tell me that you're at the Harringtons' house right now and I received a very distressing call from Dee. You need to get out of there now and meet me in the office. That is an order."

Before she could protest, Martina had hung up. She stared at the blank screen and shook her head. The day was most certainly not going as planned.

18

Selena slid the key into the lock on the lobby door. There wasn't a receptionist at Drakos Monroe on Sundays, and Martina had trusted her with a key to the office. For all Selena knew, it would be the last time she'd set foot inside the firm. Martina had never demanded she do anything. She'd always been calm, cool, and collected. But Selena could tell by her tone on the phone, she was pissed.

She didn't like the idea of making Martina upset. She loved Martina and respected her. But she sure as hell didn't like being summoned back to the office. *That's an order.* In general, she didn't like anyone telling her what to do. She thought she wanted to be like Martina and be a partner at Drakos Monroe Security and Investigations, one of the largest and most respected firms in the San Francisco Bay Area. But now she wondered if the next few years of her training would simply be taking orders from other people. She didn't like the sound of that.

She locked up behind her and continued toward her cubicle. She reached her workspace and found Martina waiting there for her. Martina demanded, "Let's go into conference room one."

Selena followed silently behind, taking orders like a good little girl. She hated it. She wanted to be the one giving orders, not taking them. She wanted the freedom to do what she thought was right. They should've questioned Julie Harrington the day Dee and Selena witnessed her meeting with Ocampo at the nail salon. Drakos Monroe was playing it too safe. If they had questioned Julie, maybe she and Brendon wouldn't be in danger. Maybe this all could've ended days ago.

They entered conference room number one, the smaller of the two conference rooms, which housed a table and four chairs. Martina shut the door behind her and ordered, "Take a seat."

Selena's pulse raced. She'd never been on Martina's bad side before. She already didn't like it. She sat in the chair and folded her hands in her lap.

Martina took the seat across from her. If Selena hadn't known better, she would've expected that at any moment steam would pour out of Martina's ears. As it was, her cheeks were red and face long. "Thank you for coming down. We have two objectives this evening. The first is for you and I to have a discussion about today's events and the other is to debrief the team."

Selena wasn't entirely clear on the specifics of those objectives, but she nodded anyways.

Martina straightened her posture. "From what I understand from the conversation with Dee and my team, you were threatened by Ocampo, then you went to confront him and then you went to confront Rick Harrington. Meetings with Ocampo and Rick were not sanctioned. You never notified me of the danger you, and now everyone around you, is in. You and I agreed all steps would be cleared through me. Do you remember making this agreement with me?"

"Yes, but—"

Martina raised her hand to silence her. "There is no excuse

for your behavior. It was dangerous, it was risky for the operation, and quite frankly, reckless. Not only did you do that, but you have now undermined my authority as a partner at this firm. If you weren't my stepdaughter, you would have been fired the second you walked through the front door."

Selena fought the tears that were threatening to be unleashed. Martina wasn't just upset, she was furious. "I'm-I'm sorry."

"Are you? Because it isn't the first time you've gone off book. How about when you almost got yourself killed at the Burlingame house? God only knows what else you've done that I just don't know about. I'm seriously wondering if I can trust you to follow the rules here. This is your final warning to follow the rules, which are checking in with me on every activity associated with the case and following the plan, like when I say don't leave your vehicle, you don't leave your vehicle. This is the last time I can cover for you. Are we clear?"

Selena sunk into her seat. She began to wonder if she was capable of following orders. She certainly didn't like to. But when a child's life was on the line, was she really expected to do nothing? She supposed as long as she worked for Martina, she would have to follow her orders.

"Yes."

Martina exhaled. "Look, I don't approve of you going rogue, but I can understand the thought process. We just can't allow that here at the firm - you're not even licensed yet. I love you and would be crushed if anything ever happened to you. Not to mention what it would be like to have to explain to your father if something happened to you. Until you have more experience, you *have* to follow the rules."

Selena nodded. From now on, she'd have to.

"Now that we have that out of the way. I have a team assembled in conference room two. I want you to tell them everything you discovered today. We have a strategy to update, one that we need your input on."

I'm not being sent home? Or taken off the case? Selena mustered every bit of courage and put on a brave face. "Okay. Let's do it."

Martina gave her a reassuring nod.

Selena followed Martina out of the conference room with her head held high and entered conference room two, the site of the meeting she'd had with Martina just the day before. This time, there were three other private investigators who clearly had set up camp in the conference room at the end of the large table.

Martina spoke to the investigators. "Team, I want to introduce you to Selena. As I mentioned earlier, she is the one who has been leading our strategy, with my assistance. This is Selena's first case, however, as you know, and as the reports have revealed, Selena has decided to go a different route today. I'm not saying I wouldn't have done the same thing, but it was risky." She turned to Selena. "However, I have a feeling you have some interesting information to share with us. You have the floor."

Selena was stunned. Martina would've done the same thing? Maybe Martina was forcing her to play it safe simply because she was her stepdaughter.

Selena stood tall, and after describing the day's events, she continued to say, "I have a few different theories about what could be going on. One, the traffickers have contacted the Harringtons and demanded ransom with instruction to not involve anyone else, which is why Mr. Harrington fired us. Maybe he said, 'drop your team or we kill the girl.' If this is the case, there's going to be another meet between the Harringtons and Ocampo. Any movement from the Harringtons or Ocampo could mean a drop. Secondary theory, Julie Harrington did in fact sell Emily to the traffickers and somehow Rick found out and is trying to get her back. There are other theories, and I'm open to hearing them, but my gut says whatever put Emily into the hands of these bad guys, there will be movement happening very soon. We need minute-by-minute reports on the Harringtons, the nail salon, and Ocampo. They will be meeting, and I think it will be our only chance to get Emily back."

She glanced over at Martina, wondering if she approved. "Martina?"

"I think your theories are sound, and I think Mr. Harrington is trying to get his daughter back. I definitely think they'll be meeting because Ocampo wants the money and Mr. Harrington wants his daughter." She glanced over at the other three in the room. "Call the teams out in the field, let them know what's going on and keep your eyes open. Report back any kind of movement from any of the targets. If one of them sneezes, I want to hear about it."

Martina glanced up at Selena. "Nice work."

Selena gave a quick head nod before sitting back down into her seat, willing herself to remain strong. The meeting definitely had gone differently than she had thought it would. She still didn't like taking orders. Would she really be a future leader at Drakos Monroe? Or should she make her own path and start her own firm, where she wouldn't have to answer to anyone?

Martina said, "My suggestion is that we stay here and wait until we hear from the field before making another move."

Selena sunk back down. She felt good about potentially bringing Emily home. But what about Brendon? They knew where he lived. Maybe they knew where she lived too. "What about Brendon and the people in my house? They could be in danger. I tend to think maybe not, but you never know."

Martina nodded. "That's a good point. I would tend to think

they wouldn't go after your roommates or Brendon, but since Brendon was threatened and these types of people don't typically fool around, let's put a security team at each location—Selena's house and Brendon's apartment. Better safe than sorry. I'll let security know. Anything else, Selena?"

Selena had been warned that being a private investigator was dangerous, but it never occurred to her that it could also be dangerous for everyone she loved. "I think that should cover it."

Selena discussed next steps with the team while Martina called in the security teams.

Three hours later, one of the team members phone's buzzed. He answered it. All Selena could see was a head bobbing before he turned off the phone. He set it down on the desk and stood up. He was tall and built like a tank. "Mr. Harrington is on the move."

Martina shot out of her seat. "Team, if this is the meet, we'll need backup. All three of you call the guys in the field. I want flak jackets on everybody. Use the utmost caution." She turned to Selena "When was the last time you were at the firing range?"

"It's been awhile, but I have my baton and I have a taser."

Martina shrugged. "They'll have to do. You'll ride with me. Get a flak jacket from the supply room. I'll grab a couple extra rounds from my office. I'll meet you in the lobby in five." Martina glanced over at the man-tank. "Denver, when you find out which direction Harrington's headed, call it in. I want a play-by-play."

"Yes, ma'am."

Another member of the team shot up from behind her computer. She was middle-aged with red, curly hair that sprung in every direction. "Just got a call. Ocampo is on the move."

Selena scanned the room. "This is it. I can feel it. It's the meet."

Martina said, "I think you're right. Lobby in five. All teams go. All comms go to Selena's cell."

Adrenaline soared through Selena. She supposed she should be afraid, but she was excited. She couldn't wait to take these guys down and get Emily back.

19

Selena stared out the window at the construction site of a new office building. It was dark, but in the distance she could see two cars with their headlights on. Martina pulled over onto the frontage road and turned off the headlights. She turned to Selena. "We need to go on foot. Are you ready for this? This could get very dangerous."

"I'm ready."

"Good. I also think you're ready. You can do this, Selena, just follow my lead. I have a firearm, you don't. Stay a pace behind and don't do anything without my direct order, do you understand?"

"Yes, I understand. Follow your orders."

They hurried along the road before taking cover behind a large trash bin. They crouched down, and Martina handed her a pair of binoculars. Selena accepted them and raised them to eye level and peered through.

Rick Harrington was carrying a large duffel bag and walking toward Benjie Ocampo. To the right of Ocampo was a very large man, likely the muscle, and he had his hands gripped on Emily Harrington's shoulders. *She was alive.*

Selena handed the binoculars back to Martina. She followed Martina's lead as they crept around the side until they were situated behind Rick's car. They waited.

Rick and Ocampo exchanged words.

Rick handed the duffle bag to Ocampo. Ocampo took it and nodded to the large man holding Emily. As Rick stepped toward Emily, Ocampo pulled a gun from the back of his trousers and aimed it at Rick Harrington. Martina whispered, "Stay here," and then darted ahead toward the men with her weapon positioned on Ocampo. Selena's heart raced as she watched the scene, peeking out from behind Rick Harrington's car.

Ocampo fired at Rick and he dropped to the ground. In a blur, six more shots were exchanged between Ocampo, the large man, and Martina. Fear shot through Selena's body as she watched Martina fall on her back. Selena didn't see any blood near Martina. *Must have hit her vest.* Ocampo and the other men were lying in a pool of their own blood. Emily ran over to her father and was now kneeling down next to him. She didn't want to defy orders, but ...

She shouted, "Martina!"

Martina waved without getting up.

The little girl turned to look at Selena but didn't leave her father.

Martina held her chest with one hand and slowly stood up. She winced and then yelled to Selena, "Take Emily back to the car, I'll call 9-1-1 and secure the scene."

Selena ran over to Rick and Emily. A groan came from the man. *He was still alive.* Martina joined them. "I'm going to call for help. Where does it hurt?"

He pointed to his shoulder. Martina initiated pressure to his shoulder with her left gloved hand and dialed 9-1-1 with the other. She looked over her shoulder to Selena. "Go ahead."

Selena met Emily's terrified gaze. "Hi Emily, my name is

Selena. Why don't you come with me, so we can be safe and wait for help, okay?"

Emily shook her head.

Rick eked out, "Go, Emily."

"Daddy!"

"Go ..."

Selena extended her hand. "It's okay, come with me. I'll carry you, since it's a ways back to the car." Selena inched closer to Emily and wrapped her arms around the girl, picked her up, and ran away from the carnage. As she ran, she explained to Emily that she was safe. The girl cried all the way to the car.

Sweat dripping down her back, Selena opened the backseat of Martina's vehicle and gently placed Emily down. The girl looked up at Selena. Her face was dirty and streaked with tears. Selena knelt down. "Are you hurt?"

She shook her head. "I want Daddy."

"The ambulance is going to come soon and fix him. We'll wait here for help to arrive, okay?"

The girl nodded.

"Are you cold?"

The girl nodded again.

Selena removed her parka and wrapped it around Emily. Emily accepted it and scooted to the seat next to her. Selena gave her a warm smile and climbed in and closed the door.

Selena pulled the phone from her pocket and called the tank, also known as Denver. "We have Emily secured. Shots were fired. Martina is okay but took a slug to the vest, she's still at the scene. She's called 9-1-1. Hopefully they get here soon. Let the rest of the team know the status. Also, can you check in with the security detail and get a status on my house and Brendon's?"

"Yes, ma'am."

She hung up and returned her attention to the small girl. "Are you hungry?"

She shook her head back and forth.

Selena hadn't spent much time with children and wasn't quite sure how to entertain her during the ordeal. She thought back to her conversation with Emily's family and teacher. "I hear you like birds."

The girl's blue eyes opened wide.

"What is your favorite bird?" Selena asked.

"I like cardinals. They're red. Red is my favorite color."

"Really? I like those too. What other birds do you like?"

As the girl continued to discuss birds, Selena heard the faint sound of sirens. Help was on the way.

20

Selena said, "Thank you," and hung up her phone. The report from the security teams tasked with watching her house and Brendon's apartment hadn't reported any suspicious activity. Relief washed over her. "Who was that?" Emily asked.

"Those were some friends letting me know that my other friends are okay."

"That's good. So, like I was saying, the California Condor has the longest wingspan of any other bird in all of North America and are often mistaken for small airplanes ..."

The kid talked non-stop about birds and for a seven-year-old, she knew a surprisingly vast amount of information about them.

Her phone buzzed again and her heart skipped a beat. She relaxed at the text from Martina.

BAD GUYS DEAD. RICK WILL BE OKAY. DRIVE OVER.

Selena sent a thumbs-up and buckled Emily in before commandeering the driver's seat. She drove the two hundred yards to the scene now surrounded by half a dozen cop cars and three ambulances. She parked and turned around to look at Emily. "We're going to go see your dad. The bad guys are gone."

Emily stared blankly at her.

Selena opened the passenger door and led Emily over to where Martina stood waving her arm.

They approached Martina, who was standing at the rear entrance of an ambulance. Selena peered over and before she could tell Emily her dad was inside, the girl ran over to the open bay and climbed up into the back. Ignoring the paramedic attending to Rick Harrington, she yelled, "Daddy!" and flung her arms around his body.

He grinned. "Hi sweetheart. I'm so happy to see you."

"I missed you so much."

Selena stood back with Martina and watched the scene. In that moment, all the danger, the worry about school, and the concern for her own well-being slipped away.

After examining both Rick and his daughter, the paramedic explained they were ready to transport Rick to the hospital to get patched up. Rick Harrington's wound was a through-and-through with likely no need for surgery, and Emily was physically unharmed, though the paramedics recommended a full exam at the hospital. *Ick.* Selena knew what that meant. But, considering what Martina and Selena had walked into, it was probably the best possible outcome. The bad guys were pronounced dead at the scene thanks to some expert marksmanship by Martina.

Rick had consented to Martina keeping Emily in their care while he was transported to the hospital and they waited for his wife to arrive from dropping off the baby at her parents' house. He must have sensed his daughter had formed quite the bond with Selena. Selena had felt it too. All she'd done was whisk Emily away from a couple bad guys and then discuss birds for nearly thirty minutes straight. The kid was obsessed with birds. Selena had no idea any one person could enjoy talking that much about birds. *Mind blown.*

Martina said, "All right, we'll meet you at the hospital. Selena, are you ready to head out?"

"Don't we need to talk to the police?"

"They'll meet us at the hospital for formal statements. I already gave them my statement and they've called the detective handling Emily's case. We can go."

Selena glanced down at Emily. "You ready to go?"

Emily nodded emphatically.

Selena, Martina, and Emily sat at the hospital cafeteria munching on French fries while Emily continued to educate them about her favorite birds. They were waiting for the call that they could bring Emily up to her father's room. Thirty minutes later, Selena's cell phone buzzed and she picked it up. "Hello, Selena Bailey."

"It's Rick Harrington, you can bring Emily now. I'm in 107A."

"Will do."

She hung up and eyed Emily. "Guess what? Your daddy is feeling better and we can go see him now."

The girl's eyes lit up.

Martina gave her a nod before taking the trays over to the trash. On the ride up in the elevator, Emily asked, "How did you know to find me?"

"We've been working with your dad and mom."

"You mean Julie? She's not my mom. She's my *stepmother*. My mom died."

Selena gazed down at her. "I'm so sorry your mom died. My mom died too."

Emily's eyes went wide. "She did? Did she have cancer?"

According to a college paper she'd written, yes, but in actuality, no. "No, a bad man hurt her. But then I got to live with my dad and my stepmother."

"Is your stepmother nice?"

Selena glanced over at Martina and felt a lump form in her throat. "She's the best."

"Do you still miss your mom even though you have a nice stepmom?"

"Yes."

Emily stared down at the floor of the elevator. "Me too."

At the ding, Emily put her small hand in Selena's and they stepped off the elevator. Selena glanced down and forced back the tears. She had been seventeen when she'd lost her mother, but Emily was only seven. Selena couldn't even begin to imagine how her life would have turned out if she'd lost her mother at that age. Her dad had still been an addict back then and he and Martina hadn't met.

They walked toward room 107A and entered. Rick Harrington was propped up with his arm in a sling with Julie Harrington sitting next to him in a chair.

Emily ran toward her father and yelled, "Daddy!" And once again flung her arms across his chest.

He grinned. "Hi sweetheart."

"You're okay now?"

There were tears in the man's eyes. Selena glanced over at Julie, who looked relieved, but apprehensive as well.

Selena wanted to be gentle in questioning the two, but she also wanted to know the truth. "Hello, Mr. Harrington, Mrs. Harrington."

Rick said, "Thank you so much, Selena and Martina, I don't know what I would've done without you. Thank you so much for bringing Emily back to us alive and saving my life."

Julie's face was flushed, and it looked like she was fighting tears. "Thank you for saving my husband's life."

"You're very welcome." Selena eyed Martina, she nodded in what looked like approval. Selena said, "The police will be here shortly to get your full statements, but I'd like to discuss a few things before we go. Maybe, Julie, you can speak with us?"

Julie glanced over at her husband and said, "Okay, we can step outside and leave you two alone." She got up from the chair next to her husband and waved them over to the doorway. "What is it?" Julie asked once they were all in the hall.

Selena tipped her head. "We know you met with Ocampo at the nail salon on Wednesday night. What is going on?"

Julie exhaled. "I'm so sorry we had to keep the secret from you, but as soon as you told us they were traffickers at the nail salon, I foolishly thought that I could try to get Emily back. That's why I met them at the nail salon. It was because I was trying to negotiate a deal. They gave us a price. It took a few days to gather the cash. We did everything they told us to do. Why did they shoot Rick?"

Martina responded with a straight face. "Because they're criminals. They can't be trusted. My guess, by killing Rick, they would get your money plus any profit from selling Emily. You should have come to us. We could have protected you."

Julie's face scrunched up. "They told us if we told anyone that they would kill her."

It was as Selena expected. Except, she'd assumed Ocampo had contacted the Harringtons for ransom, not the other way around. Julie had put herself in a lot of danger to get her stepdaughter back.

Selena said, "That was very brave, but very dangerous."

There was desperation in Julie's eyes. "I know, but I just couldn't imagine not getting Emily back. She's had such a rough go lately and then with a new baby ... We haven't given her enough attention. I just had to do everything I could. She was with me when she was taken. I had to get her back. It was my fault."

Selena put her hand on Julie's shoulder. "It wasn't your fault."

Julie had been quite forthcoming. If she were going to ask any more questions, it was the time. "Out of curiosity, why did you box up Emily's things?"

Julie shook her head as tears dropped from her eyes. "I didn't want to jinx things. I thought, maybe if I boxed things up, she'd come back. And if I put her things back the way they were then maybe it would go the other way. Murphy's Law. I don't know. It's stupid, I guess."

"I'm glad all of you are safe," Martina added.

"What about those women? At the nail salon, I mean," Julie asked.

Martina said, "When the police came to the scene, I explained what happened and what was going on at the nail salon."

"Good. You think they'll be able to save them?" Julie asked.

Martina said, "I hope so."

"Do you have any more questions? I'd like to get back to my husband."

"No, thank you."

With that, Julie Harrington rushed back in to the hospital room.

Selena and Martina also made their way to the foot of Rick Harrington's bed. Selena glanced at the three happily reunited faces. "We're going to head out. Take care of yourselves."

Emily untangled herself from her father and ran to Selena, embracing her in a hug. Selena wrapped her arms around the girl. "Take care, Emily, and every time I see a cardinal, I'll think of you."

"Thank you, Selena."

Staring down into her cherubic face, Selena had to fight the tears again. "You're welcome, Emily."

With that, Emily ran back over to her dad and stepmother. They waved as she and Martina exited the hospital room. It felt good to have a win.

Selena opened the passenger door to Martina's car and slipped in. What a day. She was exhausted and thrilled that Emily was safe and with her family. There was no better feeling in the world.

Martina started the engine and headed out of the hospital parking lot. "Great work, Selena. I have to warn you, though, they don't all end up like this. But you did good with Emily and had great instincts on the case. You'll make a fine private investigator—not that I ever had any doubt."

"Thank you."

Martina lifted her wrist and studied her watch. "My gosh, it's after ten. I think we all earned a good night's sleep tonight. I'll drop you at the office so you can pick up your car, okay?"

"Sounds good. Do you mind if I call Brendon?" She couldn't wait to hear his voice.

Martina gave her a coy smile. "Go ahead."

Selena grabbed her phone from her jacket pocket and dialed. It rang. And rang. And then his voicemail. Maybe he was already asleep? Or maybe he was studying at the library? He usually turned his phone to silent when he was in the library. He was such a boy scout. The thought made her smile. She texted him, MISS YOU. CALL ME., before tucking the phone back in her pocket.

"No word on the nail salon?" Selena asked.

"No, not yet. I'll call tomorrow and get an update. I'd like to hear if the women have been rescued."

"Me too." There were two fewer bad guys on the loose and two girls back home with their families. Saving those women would be the icing on the cake.

21

Selena woke up gasping for air with sweat running down her temples. Without getting out of bed, she reached over to her desk and pulled her phone from its charger. It was nine in the morning. There were no calls or texts from Brendon. She called him. It rang. And rang. And then it went to voicemail. She combed through her memories to remember if Brendon had ever not called or texted her back. *No*. Her heart was nearly thumping out of her chest. Maybe he hadn't seen her text after a late night of studying. *Or ...*

She jumped out of bed and threw on clothes, slid on her boots, grabbed her coat, and hurried out of the house. The morning air slapped her in the face, but she shook it off and ran to her car, parked two blocks away. She reached it, out of breath, and slid in. She turned on the engine and sped off toward Brendon's apartment. She pulled up in front, but there was no parking. She said, "Fuck it," and double-parked. She ran up to his door and pounded on it. She paced as she waited. She pounded again. A minute later, the door opened and Glenn stood there with one eye shut, wearing only a pair of red boxers. "What the hell, man?"

Selena had her hand on her hip. "Is Brendon here?"

"What? Nah. I thought he was with you."

Selena's stomach flipped. "Are you sure he's not here?"

Glenn stepped back and shrugged. "You can look."

Selena stormed in and entered Brendon's bedroom. He wasn't there. She searched the room for his backpack. It wasn't there either. She spun around and headed toward Glenn still in the hall. "When was the last time you saw him?" Selena asked with her voice raised.

"I don't know. Maybe two or three?"

"Did he have his backpack with him?"

"I think so. Dang, what time is it?"

Selena shook her head. Where could he be? Had the security team been watching Glenn, and not Brendon, all night? *Shit. Fuck. No.*

Her phone buzzed. Her heart stopped. Maybe it was him. But it was Martina. The pit in her stomach grew larger. Selena said, "I can't find Brendon—" and then went on to explain the lack of returned phone calls and how he hadn't been seen since yesterday.

"Where are you now?" Martina's voice was panicked.

"I'm at Brendon's apartment."

"I'll come get you."

Selena felt faint. "Why would you come to get me? I have my car."

Martina didn't answer.

Dread filled every cell in Selena's body.

Martina spoke. "Don't leave. I'm on my way."

Selena stood frozen, unable to speak.

"Selena?"

"Tell me."

"I'll be there in five minutes." Martina's voice cracked.

Selena shook her head back and forth as the tears streamed down her face.

"Selena?"

Glenn appeared, now wrapped in a blanket. "Dude, what's going on? Are you okay?"

Selena looked up at him. She shook her head silently. He ushered her over to the couch and sat her down. He took the phone from her hand. She let him.

"Hey, uh, who is this?" Glenn asked into the speaker.

There were muffled noises coming from her phone.

"I'm Glenn, Brendon's roommate. What's going on?"

More muffled noises.

"Oh, okay. I'll stay here." He hung up. "Martina said she'll be here in a minute."

Selena stared at the carpet. This couldn't be happening. She must be dreaming. She'd never woken up. That had to be it.

A knock on the door forced her to turn her head to the right. Glenn jumped up to open the door. Martina walked in with a grave look. Two uniformed officers followed her in.

Selena stared directly into Martina's eyes. "What?"

Martina rushed to her side on the couch. "I got a call from my contact at the San Bruno PD. They did a raid on the nail salon earlier this morning. When they arrived at the nail salon, it had been emptied with the exception of ... a body."

Selena gasped.

Martina put her hand on Selena's shoulder. "Honey, it was Brendon. I'm so sorry."

Selena felt like someone was literally ripping the heart from her chest and she couldn't breathe. *No. It couldn't be him. It couldn't.* She shook her head. "No."

"Yes, honey. I'm so sorry."

This was her fault. She'd gotten him killed.

22

Four days later, Selena stood next to Brendon's grave as the preacher spoke about dust and ashes and other bullshit, she wasn't sure what, she'd stopped listening minutes ago. This hadn't been divine intervention. It was the result of her recklessness and the trafficker's wrath. She felt empty, like a shell of who she once was. Any chance for love or happiness had washed away. She willed herself to not shed any more tears. In the previous days there were many, but then she realized she needed to stop feeling sorry for herself and take action. For Brendon. For the other victims.

"You ready to go to the reception?" Martina asked with pity in her eyes.

Selena watched as the other funeral attendees descended the hill to their vehicles. She shook her head. "I don't want to go." She couldn't face his family. She couldn't face any of them. She'd gotten the only man she'd ever truly loved, killed. She'd taken away a man full of promise and hope. She could barely face her own reflection. She glanced up at Martina and her Dad. "Can we just go home?"

Her father put his arm around her. "Of course."

Selena walked back to the car with her head down, wondering why there was so much ugliness in the world. Why did the monsters have to exist? Why did they have to take the people she loved?

They reached the car and Selena paused before she turned around to gaze at Brendon's final resting place. Her heart ached and her knees weakened. Why did they have to take him? She didn't know, but one thing she knew for sure was that she wouldn't ever let it happen again. Her heartbreak and the knowledge that monsters were still out there would fuel her mission to stop them. This would be *her time to rise*, not theirs.

A NOTE FROM H.K. CHRISTIE

Another awful reality: *human trafficking*. As mentioned in the story, it is absolutely everywhere. I was born and raised in the San Francisco Bay Area and was shocked, when I started my research, and found how rampant it is here *and* the rest of the United States *and* throughout the rest of the world. Not to mention, I had assumed, like many people, that human trafficking was mostly women and girls intended for the sex trade. I had no idea all genders and ages are being trafficked and forced into modern-day slavery in multiple service industries. It is horrific.

The Polarisproject.org is a an organization dedicated to:

"Serving victims and survivors through the National Human Trafficking Hotline. Building a dataset that illuminates how human trafficking really works, in real time. Turning knowledge into targeted systems-level strategies to disrupt and prevent human trafficking."

U.S. National Human Trafficking Hotline. **1-888-373 -7888** or **Text "BeFree" 233733**

If you would like to learn more or donate to the cause, please visit their website at polarisproject.org.

THANK YOU!

Thank you for reading *On The Rise*! I hope you enjoyed reading it as much as I did writing it. If you did, I would greatly appreciate if you could post a short review.

Reviews are crucial for any author and can make a huge difference in visibility of current and future works. Reviews allow us to continue doing what we love, *writing stories*. Not to mention, I would be forever grateful!

To leave a review, go to the Amazon or other webpage for *On The Rise* and scroll down to the bottom of the page to the review section. It will read, "Share your thoughts with other customers," with a button below that reads, "Write a customer review." Click the "Write a customer review" button and write away!

Thank you!

ALSO BY H.K. CHRISTIE

The Selena Bailey Novella Series

If you like thrilling twists, dark tension, and smart and driven women, then you'll love this suspenseful series featuring a young Selena Bailey and her turbulent path to becoming a top notch kickass private investigator.

Not Like Her, Book 1

One In Five, Book 2

On The Rise, Book 3

The Unbreakable Series

The Unbreakable Series is a heart-warming women's fiction series, inspired by true events. If you like journeys of self-discovery, wounded heroines, and laugh-or-cry moments, you'll love the Unbreakable series.

We Can't Be Broken, Book 0

Where I'm Supposed To Be, Book 1

Change of Plans, Book 2

JOIN H.K. CHRISTIE'S READER'S CLUB

Join my reader club to be the first to hear about upcoming novels, new releases, giveaways, promotions, and more!

It's completely free to sign up and you'll never be spammed by me, you can opt out easily at any time.

To sign up go to
www.authorhkchristie.com

ABOUT THE AUTHOR

H.K. Christie is the author of compelling stories featuring unbreakable women.

When not working on her latest novel, she can be found eating & drinking with friends, running slowly, or playing with her rescue pup, Mr. Buddy Founders.

She is a native and current resident of the San Francisco Bay Area and a two time graduate of Saint Mary's College of California.

authorhkchristie.com

ACKNOWLEDGMENTS

I'd like to thank my *Super* beta readers: Juliann Brown, Jennifer Jarrett and Anne Kasaba. Thank you for the continued encouragement, support, and invaluable feedback. I appreciate the time and effort you put into your review. Thank you!

Thank you to Nicole Nugent for the copy edit.

I'd like to thank Suzana Stankovic who designed the cover. You did an amazing job with the cover - as you always do. Thank you!

Last, but certainly not least, a special thank you to my husband, Jon. He reads (and proofs) all of my books, gives me endless encouragement, and is always trying to help in some way (from being my own personal bartender to finding ways to enrich my writing). I'm definitely lucky to have found him all those years ago. So, Mr. Christie, I thank you and I love you.

Made in the USA
Columbia, SC
26 February 2022

56872330R00079